DIAMONDS
AND
STONES

Navreet Sran is a novelist-cum-wanderer. Despite a dread for numbers, Navreet completed her bachelor's degree in accounting from GNDU, India. Thereafter, she moved to Toronto to pursue marketing from Humber College, and then went on to study event marketing at Seneca College. Currently, she is Event Coordinator for GDG Cloud Toronto, a networking group sponsored by Google. She speaks regularly at various Canadian fora on issues related to working women and on career challenges faced by South Asian women.

Her favourite pastimes are exploring different cuisines, collecting stones during riverside walks, and photography. She lives in Ontario.

Reach her at: Twitter: @navreet_sran_, Insta: @navreet_sran and Facebook: navreetsran.author

DIAMONDS AND STONES

An Unlikely Story

NAVREET SRAN

Published by
Rupa Publications India Pvt. Ltd 2023
7/16, Ansari Road, Daryaganj
New Delhi 110002

Sales centres:
Prayagraj Bengaluru Chennai
Hyderabad Jaipur Kathmandu
Calcutta Mumbai

Copyright © Navreet Sran 2023

This is a work of fiction. Names, characters, places and incidents are either the product of the author's imagination or are used fictitiously and any resemblance to any actual person, living or dead, events or locales is entirely coincidental.

All rights reserved.

No part of this publication may be reproduced, transmitted, or stored in a retrieval system, in any form or by any means, electronic, mechanical, photocopying, recording or otherwise, without the prior permission of the publisher.

P-ISBN: 978-93-5702-164-7
E-ISBN: 978-93-5702-397-9

First impression 2023

10 9 8 7 6 5 4 3 2 1

The moral right of the author has been asserted.

Printed in India

This book is sold subject to the condition that it shall not, by way of trade or otherwise, be lent, resold, hired out, or otherwise circulated, without the publisher's prior consent, in any form of binding or cover other than that in which it is published.

One

How stupid do you have to be to do something that you certainly know is wrong? An identical thought crossed their minds at the same time as they stared at each other across the breakfast table. Each could provide a different reason for harbouring such a thought; for his part, Mr Sharma could not believe his sensible daughter was considering resigning from the job he had hooked her up after so much hassle. He'd almost staked his friendship with Ajeet to get her in; Ajeet hadn't taken well to Mr Sharma's sudden interest in his ex-wife's company. Mr Sharma's prying had reopened old wounds and things had taken a good deal of time to settle down again. But young Meera evidently didn't understand the worth of time, money or anything. In fact, she seemed set on ruining all her father's efforts. *It's crap from movies in her head. Nonsense radicals and their motivations.* Mr Sharma shook his head, cursing the monolithic force of Western culture yet again.

Meera, however, believed that she had been stupid to accept this job in the first place. Her father had placed her under Namita's wing so she couldn't fly away from home in search of another job.

'So you feel that your job is not exciting?' Mr Sharma pulled out one of the flimsier reasons Meera had flung on the table so far, and his words prickled her exactly the way he'd wanted them to. She inhaled deep and bit the inside of her lower lip. He saw the lines of her forehead crease in submission, marking the steps towards his victory. He was certainly not everyone's cup of coffee, especially not hers.

'What excitement do you expect? People work to make a living.' He looked at his wife for affirmation.

'Of course,' Mrs Sharma said, slipping into the chair next to him. 'Do you even realize how many people only dream of this job? You're lucky you never saw those long interview queues.'

Mr Sharma looked at both women. He had perhaps expected a more stalwart defence from his wife.

'That's what I'm saying, mom. I don't deserve it,' said Meera. 'I don't think Namita has ever liked me either. Every time she looks at me, it reminds me of how I got in here. I'll never make it to her list of the best, no matter how hard I try.'

Mr Sharma gave a sly smile. His beady eyes swung towards his daughter, while his sparsely covered skull stayed still. Controlled and confident, he said, 'You should make her like you then. Prove to her that you're worthy. Instead of quitting, you should think about a promotion.'

There he goes again, Meera thought, watching her attempts finally collapsing. She'd wanted to put better explanations on the table, but she knew deep down that they wouldn't have worked either. She looked blankly at the plate for a few seconds and then picked up the spoon, poking vaguely at a vacant side of her plate. Helplessness and disgust eclipsed the charm of her young face as she straightened hair behind her ears, letting it flow down her back over her striped blue formal shirt.

Mrs Sharma pulled the chopping board towards her and began slicing potatoes to go with the carrots she'd diced a while ago. She had cared less and less for these discussions within her family since she'd accepted that her husband would make the choices for her children. At once, she remembered the bowl of eggs. She rose from her seat to uncover the bowl on the other side of table.

'You want an egg? I boiled a few,' she said, passing them to Meera. Her daughter looked at her in disbelief and finished her breakfast without another word. Mr Sharma, though, plucked an egg from the bowl.

He did not like Meera's defiance, even if it was directed at the eggs. He strongly wanted to object. But after seeing her morose condition, he decided to relent. If he had begun, the opening line, like for most of his other sermons, would've been 'when I was your age', leading to a climactic account of his childhood greatness. Of course, Meera doubted the authenticity of these stories, but she never dared question them.

Meera rose from her chair a few minutes later to grab her laptop and handbag. 'All right, I should go,' the girl said coldly, looking right through her parents.

Mr Sharma glanced through his thick spectacles. 'I can drive you to work. I'm heading that way,' he said hoarsely.

But the girl had already marched towards the door.

'I'm fine,' she replied calmly and shut the door behind

her. This, she knew, would not be ignored; he would get her back in the evening. For now, though, he merely watched her angry departure.

Mr and Mrs Sharma had a reputation to uphold. They were one of those tough couples who'd been born into the middle class but worked their way upwards to upper middle class. This accomplishment was something that Mrs Sharma never forgot to talk about with her sisters, especially the two who had married into average households in Dehradun. It took Kundan Sharma years of exertion to establish his real estate firm in south Delhi, which he'd crafted single-handedly, starting with nothing but a small chunk of land from back home that he'd traded off to make his first investment in Delhi. Many who insisted that Kundan's success was only due to the spontaneous boom in the economy also believed that not every investor could survive the recession that had followed it. But Kundan had not only survived, he had thrived, cementing his reputation as a shrewd businessman.

He'd secured the best possible education, lifestyle and facilities for his kids. They'd gone to the best private school in Delhi, learned three languages, joined sports teams, and had (mostly) kept away from bad company. As twins, Meera and her brother Sunny had nothing in common in terms of demeanour, behaviour or their roles in the family. Mr Sharma focused on the three things that he believed would best generate profit, and did so in exacting proportion: his business, his son, and himself.

When his son had wanted to join an expensive aviation academy, he'd paid the enormous training fees for 'his boy' to obtain a licence. Things were, however, rather different when Meera expressed the same desire. Her plea had been tactfully denied. She was told to focus on her MBA; piloting was not a good career choice. She wasn't surprised. As matter of fact, she knew that her father wouldn't agree, as the programme involved huge investments of time and money and, therefore, accepted her father's decision. Mrs Sharma had silently admired her daughter's meekness, as this was exactly how she wanted Meera to be: sensible, well behaved and compliant.

Two

'SP' held the door of the office elevator as soon as he spotted Meera sprinting through the reception gallery. The abbreviation had nothing to do with him being a superintendent of police—he wasn't—it stood for Shanti Prakash Verma, an outdated Banarasi name that didn't go with his current lifestyle, nor did it suit his city-bred girlfriend, Akshita.

'Thanks,' Meera said, panting while making room for herself at the back of the packed elevator. SP winked at her as he stepped in and the door slid to automatically shut itself.

Mrs Banerjee, an older and seasoned employee, sighed from within the elevator, frowning at Meera and SP. 'Late again!'

Meera smiled nervously. 'There was an insane rush at the platforms and all the trains were tightly packed,' she said and paused, trying to lean forward and make herself visible to Mrs Banerjee, hoping it would draw attention to the fact that her back was pressing Meera against the elevator wall.

'Well, nothing can be done. It is what it is during rush hours. One must depart early, child,' Mrs Banerjee replied, merely tilting her head while her body remained still.

SP tossed Meera a wicked smile as he remained squished against the control panel. In fact, each person in the five-by-five box stood uncomfortably, holding their breath. On the seventh floor, three disembarked, and the others quickly spread their tense limbs.

'Did you hear about Varun's transfer?' SP asked Meera as they walked out of the elevator on the tenth floor. She looked at him, a bit startled, and noticed a menacing smile on his tanned face. It was as if he was spilling news that until now had been contained within the closed cabins of management.

Meera lowered her voice as they approached their department. 'Didn't Varun join two months back? He didn't like it here or what?'

'Rather the opposite. The place didn't like him,' SP said, punching the time machine. 'He was too nosy, you know. Screwed it up with his overenthusiasm during the Chennai project. I tried to warn him. It doesn't matter how good you are at something; things are eventually going to happen according to that witch's way. Besides, Namita has nothing else going on in her life but this business—how can anyone hope to compete with her.'

He pulled a cup of coffee from the vending machine; Meera followed, repeating his every action. She poured coffee into her cup, giving SP an affirmative look, appearing like just another naïve listener, cowering in the intellectual shade of an experienced colleague.

SP sneaked into his cubicle and arranged his stuff on his desk; Meera did the same in her cubicle.

He said, turning on his computer, 'Anyway, big news is I'm getting engaged next Saturday.'

'Wow…that's so early!' she whispered, excited and shocked simultaneously.

'Akshita's family picked the date. Some astrology stuff, she says. I couldn't negotiate. It *has* to be next week. I need at least three days off to arrange stuff,' he said.

'Congrats!' Meera exclaimed. 'I should've figured out that devilish smile earlier.' She chuckled over the low-parting wall.

'Shush…later, later,' he whispered.

'Come on, everyone should know.'

'Not today. I have no money to treat fifty people to samosas.' He peered up at the camera atop his head.

Meera peered, a coy smile playing on her lips. 'But you will treat me, won't you?'

'Of course,' SP said nervously and then the two turned to their screens.

∞

Three hours into work, Meera was already fed up. It was exasperating to have to ogle at the computer screen when the back of her head was aching so relentlessly. An erratic muscle strain ran throughout her body. She looked at the clock and then the glass window facing a highway. The cars racing in their lanes resembled a scene from some video game. She closed her eyes, having trouble figuring out which part of her body was suffering the most; her brain seemed to be the most likely answer.

She reproached herself over and over. There were a couple

of justifications she could've given her father this morning, and she had practised them well through the night, but they would not have stood against his intense gaze. She sighed, knowing well that she had no plan, nor was she enough of a crackpot to hurt her family's reputation (or indeed her own) by doing something imprudent. She wished her brother Sunny would be of some help but he, like their mother, laughed at most of Meera's business ideas.

Ramlal, a weasel-like office boy, thumped a stash of papers down upon Meera's desk. 'Ma'am has called you into her office,' he said, making sure he was heard by all.

Meera looked up at the camera, suddenly feeling certain that she knew the reason for the call. She'd done nothing worthwhile for the past two hours and had instead swiftly spun a pen between her fingers and moved her chair, to and fro, across her cubicle. She rose and headed down the aisle, passing some fifteen cubicles on either side, and continuing through the long corridor, up to the elevator. In five minutes or so, she was at Namita's door. This walk was one among several other unnerving walks she'd made since her recruitment, especially as she had no idea what work she was supposed to have done by now. She closed her eyes and tried to remember statistical figures from the file she'd glanced at a minute ago, but it was all a mess, and nothing could be fairly reckoned from it. She gave up this last-ditch attempt and accepted that she'd have to be honest about her ignorance.

Namita's voice beckoned her through the glass door. She held her breath and stepped in.

The lady sat as smartly and squarely as ever in her carbon-grey suit. Her head leaned against her phone as she gestured for Meera to hang on. Silently, the girl ogled the recently renovated interior of Namita's office, which was white and grey and thinly outlined with black at the table edges. There was a row of crystal vases and vintage statues on a ledge behind her chair. On the varnished wooden desk was a white laptop with the Apple logo emblazoned on it, and a staggered glass chandelier hung above, casting a soft light on everything.

The best and worst thing about Namita Shah was that she could always dish out witticisms with a smile, which would make any person in front of her look at the ground, momentarily confused.

'How're you doing, my girl?' asked Namita, looking up as she disconnected the call.

Meera took a few steps forward. 'Morning, Ma'am.'

Namita wore an artificial smile on her face as her eyes scanned Meera's nervous frame. 'So got an invitation for your friend's engagement?' she began capriciously.

'Invitation? For what?' Meera stuttered.

'Frogs sing their hearts out before anyone else can guess that rains are visiting the jungle,' Namita scoffed. 'I like such happy souls.'

Meera looked at the ground.

Namita stood up, her polished high heels gleaming, and walked to the other side of the desk. Standing next to Meera, she started comparing her height closely with Meera's. Suddenly, her expression altered; she now had a minute frown upon her forehead. 'Your friend SP has asked for three days off next week. I'm sure he expects your help with shopping and preparations.'

Meera shrugged. 'He hasn't mentioned anything yet, but

he might catch up after work.'

'Might?' Namita mocked. 'He can skip a meal but will not skip chattering with you. Anyway, I just saw you sitting confused at your desk and so wondered if I could help in any way. You know what a tight schedule we're on—the audit's coming up.' Namita said, spinning the miniature crystal globe on her desk. 'Every single minute matters, Meera. I hope we're on the same page,' she stressed her words, waving her right palm.

Meera spoke sincerely, her forehead creasing. 'I understand, Ma'am.'

'In that case, dear, you should not think of celebrations right now. We've much more important things to sort. I need to see the tradelines report before lunch,' Namita said, smiling and rotating the globe again.

Meera nodded while mentally calculating the time the report would actually take her to finish. Namita paused the miniature and glanced at her.

'Is there anything else we need to talk about?' Namita said, grinning at Meera, who seemed to be in a state of disarray.

A lot, Meera thought, *there's a lot we need to talk about, but you won't understand that being an office assistant and reading heaps of data isn't something I can be passionate about. Yes, I'm passionate about writing a resignation letter in a thick font, perhaps Broadway or Cooper—whichever suits your eyesight.*

'I was just, err, not feeling well. Headache and nausea. I might have to leave early today,' she said, almost slurring.

Namita's smile died and her big mascara-streaked eyes began examining Meera. 'Submit the report and we'll see. You may rest in the staffroom for a while—if you want to.'

But Namita's expression did not match her words. Meera cursed herself inwardly for such a lame excuse; she could never outsmart Namita, especially not with such unconvincing pleas.

'Okay, I should get back to work now.' Meera chuckled nervously and left the room as quickly as she could, not able to look into the woman's eyes a moment longer.

∞

Fluorescent strips glowed in one corner of the office. It was quarter past eight, and all the other lights had been switched off. The office had emptied out at around six. Meera moved her fingertips over the keyboard and the rattling of keys ruptured the absolute silence of the office. She shrank into her chair, eyes still on the screen and sipped from her travel mug, within which green tea had been sitting, ignored for more than an hour. The cold tea brought an unpleasant wrinkle between her eyes and she placed the mug back on the table. The tradelines report had been submitted at lunch, but Namita had handed her another pair of files meant for both SP and Meera that needed to be finished before the end of next week.

Her cell phone chimed.

It was a call from Sunny. She ignored it and continued fiddling with the keyboard. When the cell phone chimed again with a series of text messages, she knew that her impatient brother was downstairs, waiting for her. She sighed and saved the files before shutting down her computer. While pressing stationeries inside the drawer, a fountain pen leaked ink on her hands. But she didn't waste any time heading to the restroom since it would have only added to her brother's anxiety.

She crossed a line of barren cubicles. The spring lock on the door clacked behind her. The sound was followed by the clatter of her heels, which broke the quiet of the marbled staircase. It wasn't hard for her to guess that their mother had ordered Sunny to pick her up, otherwise he would never give rides to anyone.

When she emerged from the building, she saw Sunny waiting on the other side of the road. She looked out for cars before sprinting across the road and quickly slid into the passenger seat.

'Ten minutes? Really?' he grunted.

She glanced at her brother's neat car and new fragrance ornament. 'I had to shut down the system and get across the two-lane highway in heels,' she retorted sharply.

'That stupid gatekeeper doesn't let me park on the other side,' Sunny muttered, shifting gears as high beams from the oncoming traffic reflected the features of his face, especially his pronounced nose and lips, which were just like his twin sister's. *He seems tired*, Meera figured, and toned down her pitch.

'Mom said you haven't been answering her calls all day. She's worried,' he said.

'I dropped her a text. Doesn't that count? She keeps calling over and over.'

Sunny smiled. 'How many calls?'

'Seventeen,' Meera said, holding her forehead.

'Still better. I got thirty-two by the time I landed on the runway,' he said.

'How was your flight?' she enquired, looking at his face.

'Just got home, didn't sleep well last night and now this crazy traffic,' he said sourly. 'I can't wait to get out of this private company. It isn't the flights that drain me, but the policies—check loading, fuel, fill out records—I feel like I spend more time running checks than I do flying.'

'Paperwork is a part of the job, but if this training hurts, you can always give up and stick your ass behind a desk at dad's agency,' she said, smiling.

'I'd rather fly at a private company my entire life than work with him,' Sunny scoffed and then paused. 'You shouldn't have spoken to them that way this morning. I don't want to come back and hear of these absurd theatrics when I'm out for days at a time, and it's the second time this week.'

'I never call to bother you, they do!' she said, playing with a stray lock of hair. 'See how they sent you today to pick me up, as if I'd wander off or get lost. I'm twenty-four, but they treat me like a five-year-old.' She sighed, peering out at the tall buildings along the Delhi–Gurugram Expressway.

'It's because you don't act like you're twenty-four. They would listen if you'd talk wisely to them, but instead you're behind a suit of armour, living in your thoughts,' Sunny said, his voice louder than he'd perhaps intended.

'I've tried enough. They've only moved out of the village physically, but their way of thinking hasn't changed a bit. And damn, Sunny, will you slow down?!'

Meera wished dimly that she was able to talk to her parents the way she talked to her sibling.

He glanced at her pale face and finding her slipping back inside her armour, he said softly, 'You should just learn to let go of things.'

Meera said nothing, and the silence was likely good for both of them. Sunny didn't want to push her—he certainly didn't want to hear again about how she'd given up her dreams for him. She'd been the first to show an interest in flying, while Sunny had barely thought of it. She was the scholarly and focused one. Or, at least, she had been. Until recently.

Three

When the stars of fate decide to flip, they don't take more than a minute. It took Meera and Sunny a little longer to accept that the figure in their living room was real and not an illusion. It *was* Aniket Saxena.

The lamp in the vestibule was dim, but they could see the large schnozz, small, cheerful eyes, and the wide cheeks of the familiar guest as he rose from the couch to meet them. His natural tan had paled to the point where one could not guess at his Indian origin. The curly hair that Meera had known to be thick with dirt and twigs was finely straightened now, but the long scar running down the left side of his forehead hadn't lightened and appeared as it had fifteen years ago.

'What a surprise, brother!' Sunny threw himself upon Aniket as Mr and Mrs Sharma appeared next to their guest in the living room.

Aniket replied cheerfully, 'You've grown so tall, huh. Beard and all!'

Sunny gaped at his childhood friend. 'And look at you, suit and cravat! Your hair, what've you done to it?'

'I look more human now?' said Aniket, grinning, and

then glanced towards Meera. 'Meera, right?' he enquired.

Meera stood, unreceptive, as she always was around new people. Aniket wasn't a completely new person, but a lot had changed since he'd left Dehradun and emigrated to the US along with his family during middle school.

He smiled and held out his hand towards her. She responded with an identical smile and took a glance at his crisp, white formal shirt and dark blue pants. A fat black suitcase leaned to the side of the couch and the subtle smell of expensive cologne lingered in the air.

'You've got something on your face,' Aniket said, noticing the smear of blue ink.

She held up her stained fingers and trying to wipe the ink clear, mumbled, 'Must've happened at work.'

'You're pretty much the same.' He chuckled and looked a little longer at her face; longer than he had looked at the others. She did not reply, but smiled nervously, exposed to a big rusty box of childhood memories.

Mr Sharma walked up and wrapped his arm fondly around Meera's shoulders. 'She's a big girl now, won't come crying to us,' he said and laughed. His big nasty brain seemed to be working towards some plan, and each family member could clearly read it. Mr Sharma never showed affection unless there was some purpose to it.

Mrs Sharma was as uncertain as the children, but she knew how to follow her husband's lead; she didn't need to assess his intentions. She joined him and uttered a few sweet remarks about the past, smiling at the three reunited friends.

∞

Meera and Sunny stood on the balcony late in the evening, peering out at the distant moon and the humming city beneath them. Sunny took out a cigarette from the pocket of his pyjama—the one he had emptied and filled with cannabis.

'Everyone's asleep?' He looked around.

Meera nodded and he lit the roll.

'You knew Aniket was coming?' she asked.

Sunny took a long puff. His eyes partly shut as he savoured it for a moment and then blew the smoke out from the balcony. The odour rose sharply in the air despite his efforts.

He spoke listlessly. 'I didn't know. I'm surprised too. I just know that he called dad this afternoon while he was heading for Dehradun from the airport and our *generous* host invited him for dinner.' He paused and glanced at Meera. 'I think he's here to sell off the family house and his land in the village. There's no other reason for this visit after fifteen years.'

Meera rolled her eyes. 'So, Kundan Sharma is going to snoop into the sale? But Saxena uncle would've called him earlier if he wanted his help.'

'I don't know. I heard Aniket talking to a contractor who's interested in buying part of the land next to the highway for some town plaza project. Dad doesn't need to do much; the boy has his set-up,' Sunny said.

Meera laughed. 'Of course, he never arrives unprepared. I remember how he used to cheat in tests back in school!'

'And the day he came unprepared! I'll never forget him snatching my answer sheet during the maths exam—not returning it until there were only five minutes left. Damn, I had my lungs in my mouth the whole time!'

Meera's smile faded. 'You remember how he broke the

bell of my bicycle and never apologized?'

'That pink bicycle? I broke it! It was because your bicycle looked brand new while ours were all wobbly and junk by then,' Sunny said, artfully disposing of his cigarette. He pulled a minty gum out from the same pocket and popped it into his mouth.

The confession leaped around Meera's skull, first as a shock and then quickly turned to anger. 'I'll tell mom about your smoking,' she said coldly, turning around to leave.

'Hey, wait, I can apologize now!' Sunny moaned, still chewing his peppermint gum as he followed Meera inside.

∞

At sunrise, Aniket left in a rented car with Mr Sharma, who had decided to take a day off from work to help his guest assess the long-empty property in the Doon Valley. While he flexed his professionalism by negotiating prices with local agents, Aniket barely showed any enthusiasm, since the fluctuation of thousands (or even lakhs) of rupees wouldn't affect the round dollar value of the property that he'd calculated in his head. He was more thrilled to see Chamasari again. He'd spent the most relaxed years of his life in this tiny hillside village, about eight and a half miles to the north of Dehradun.

Mr Sharma pushed open the old creaky door of the house and Aniket strolled around the vast courtyard in the front. Gently, he touched the stark wall and wooden fence beyond which lay vacant fields in the distance. A relaxed smile surpassed the jetlag and stress otherwise saturating his face.

The garage seemed humid, and Aniket peered at the

rusted rims of his bicycle, his father's toolkit (which Aniket remembered using for various experiments of his own), and his old cricket bat, which was home to some hundred termites now. He picked up a geometry box and tried to reckon its age.

'Rain has done a lot of damage to the house, son. We might not get a good price,' Mr Sharma said from the front of the garage, peering up at the metal roof.

Aniket ducked out from the garage and said, 'I know—renovations are going to cost a lot. What would you suggest?'

'Well, it might hurt, but one thing to consider is demolishing the house and selling off the plot alone. Vacant land would fetch a better price than this wreck,' said Mr Sharma with his best real estate agent voice, complete with thoughtful frowns and gestures. Aniket suppressed a smile and looked around at the bougainvillea vines climbing the courtyard fence. It was even prettier than he remembered. He walked ahead, tempted to pluck a flower, and was reminded of his grandfather, who always used to scold him for picking from the flowerbeds.

'I think I need some time to think about it,' Aniket said, standing on his toes. He began to pluck flower after flower from the vine, until he had cradled a bouquet of pink and white blooms in his arms.

∞

Three different vegetable curries were made for lunch and the finest crockery sets were taken out—ones that, for years, had served only as decorations inside Mrs Sharma's prized glass cabinet. They smelled a little musty, but had been washed well; in fact, washed twice.

Mrs Sharma was dressed in her newly-stitched pink suit. Her hair was in a perfect bun and her lips were stained with a light peach shade. Even now, she was a blessed beauty, and only after a minute of make-up, looked much younger than her age. Mr Sharma had insisted on taking his new shirts out, which had been ironed and hung up in his closet.

'Looking beautiful, aunty. Going out somewhere?' Aniket said sluggishly to Mrs Sharma as he rolled into the kitchen in a casual T-shirt and shorts.

'No, it's just...' Mrs Sharma began.

'Yes,' Meera snapped. 'They're going to the temple.'

'Yes, we are,' Mr Sharma said, marching into the kitchen. He looked sharp in his suit and with his grey hair dyed a tough black. He had a big smile on his face. He looked different. 'You seem tired from the journey, son. Take a shower; you'll feel better,' he suggested.

'I'm fine, uncle. Might sleep for a few more hours... jetlagged.'

'I understand,' Mr Sharma said and laughed, while Aniket peered at him, a little confused.

Meera shook her head, barely believing her ears. If one of his own children had expressed such a sentiment—to go back to sleep—they'd have been hit with the much-told story of how, when their father was young, he would never sleep more than five hours a day.

Aniket turned to Meera. 'So you're not going to work?'

She glanced at him. 'It's an off'.

'Oh I see.' He cleared his throat and looked away.

'Why don't you show him around the city, Meera? The

weather is good,' Mr Sharma said, smiling and nodding at his daughter.

Meera looked at her mother, who too was beaming at her. She frowned, suddenly realizing the fantasies her parents were projecting: arranged marriage.

'That's a lovely idea. Take him out,' Mrs Sharma said.

Aniket added, 'Yeah, okay. I haven't seen Delhi.'

Meera nodded, looking askance at her folks.

∞

Mrs Sharma followed Meera into her room, clearly excited. Then, throwing open her cupboard, skimmed through Meera's clothes without preamble.

'That's all?' she exclaimed, throwing dresses, blouses and pants aside. 'You can't wear *any* of these boring manly clothes.'

'Mom, they're formals.' Meera's voice was grim. She pulled her mother away from the cupboard. 'Why are you doing this?'

'Doing what? Aniket is a good boy, and we know his family well. What's the harm in imagining the two of you together?' Mrs Sharma kept her voice casual, but jerked her wrists off from Meera's grip.

'I don't see him as a partner. I mean, he's a good person, but I can't marry a childhood friend. Besides, I'm not ready to get married anyway,' Meera said, avoiding her mother's eyes.

Mrs Sharma rolled her eyes. 'So when will you be ready? Your dad and I had two kids by your age. Give it a try. Talk to him.'

'I've never questioned your decisions, but this isn't about an MBA or a job. I can't push myself to do this just like that.'

Mrs Sharma's smile vanished. 'We've never decided anything wrong for you.' She turned back to the cupboard. 'When I met your father, I was nervous too. It's natural. Things will get better with time.' She tossed a suit upon the bed—a loose pink knee-length shirt and trouser with embroidered neon flowers that Meera had picked out for a cousin's wedding six years ago. Even though it wasn't her style any more, she couldn't care about it in the middle of such turmoil.

'That's what *you've* always done. Waited and hoped for things to be okay. Dad's life would be the same even if *you* hadn't married him; someone else would be looking after and cooking for him. You want me to be like *you*?'

Mrs Sharma stared at Meera. Her lips trembled as she tried to speak. She clutched the side of the closet as if someone had punched her chest. 'Your father was right about your tongue,' she said at last. 'Where did you even learn to speak like this?' With that, she slammed the cupboard door and marched out of the room, leaving Meera alone.

Four

The fog lifted as the sun rose in the afternoon sky, the light curling laggardly through the cold, hazy morning. The air was fresh, mixed with the scent of peanuts roasting in a vendor's cart on the corner of the street, beating the charm of popcorn and sesame balls in the cart next to it. Meera unlocked her father's car and sat in the driver's seat. Aniket sat beside her. She peeped at him from the corner of her eye and then steered the car out of the parking lot. The more she looked at her over bright, over-ethnic and floppy outfit, she regretted not questioning her mother's choice of outfit when she'd the chance to. She kept her neck taut and drew confidence from her tall, slender frame. Her often-praised Garhwali features had helped compensate for her dressing sense many times.

'It's so different from our village,' Aniket said, looking out of the window.

'It is,' she said passively, driving through the thick traffic.

He reached out and twisted the temperature knob down to nineteen. 'So, where are we going first?'

'Akshardham temple?' she said, pausing briefly. 'You like architecture?'

'Absolutely. In fact, I wanted to join an architecture school in New York earlier but for some reason I couldn't.' He glanced at her, poised to continue but when Meera said nothing, he slumped back into his seat with a slight smirk on his lips.

Meera's reclusive behaviour did not offend him; he knew what she was like. He glanced at her, eyeing her outfit, and smiled to himself. The girl caught on immediately. She inhaled deeply and tried to act cool, but she could feel her hands tighten around the steering wheel and eyes blink frequently.

He looked away.

For the next five minutes, they sat in silence, deprived of music, radio and conversation. Meera felt the air inside the car piercing through her skin; low temperatures were his habitat, not hers. Her nose, fingers and forehead became cold and numb as she cursed her father's choice yet again. *We've nothing in common, not even the most basic things like temperature!* She shook her head. *Dad has gone crazy; the people he knew in Dehradun have changed far too much to align with our current lifestyle.*

'Watch out!' Aniket exclaimed as a biker overtook them.

Meera shuddered and balanced the car in her lane. 'It's all right.'

'He could've been killed. Note down his number, Meera,' Aniket shouted.

Meera sighed. 'You don't have to deal with this. He'll be all right.'

He rattled. 'But this idiot must be taught a lesson.'

She glared at him and then stared back at the lane. Her

lips, reluctant to reply or explain anything, stayed stuck together. This sort of thing, after all, was normal on Delhi roads. She drove, cold and quiet, and eventually, Aniket lapsed into a sulky silence.

Meera leaned against the side of her car, peering up at India Gate as purple lights embraced the colossal structure in the partly dark evening sky. Aniket remained in his seat, munching on popcorn and following Meera's gaze as the yellow-red sandstone swam in yet another shifting light.

'It's pretty,' he said.

Meera looked at him. 'It is.'

'How often do you come here?' he enquired.

'Schedules are usually too tight to consider life.' She smiled.

He chuckled. 'Well, it's the same in every corner of the world. No work, no money, no life.'

She sighed. 'Don't you think it would've been different if we had all stayed in Dehradun, relying on oilseed and soybean crops?'

'You miss the village?' He smiled.

'Don't you?'

'Who wouldn't miss his birthplace? One would only be lying if he denies it, especially if he has gone so far away that coming back is nothing but an unfeasible thing now.' He tossed out a heavy breath.

Meera gazed at him, surprised.

'Settling down in a new country, building everything

from scratch—it's difficult, Meera. Those initial years were tough on us. As soon as dad's project finished, he had to look for ways to extend his US visa, and the first job that mom could find without good English and a social security number was as a cleaning lady at a restaurant.' He stared at her, his characteristic humour gone.

'What about your uncle? He didn't come to help his sister?' Meera said.

'My mother, you know, she doesn't like asking. Besides, the recession was awful all over the States back in those days. Uncle couldn't have done much anyway. Dad slogged at several companies with his résumé until he finally quit to work at a gas station: selling cigarettes and lottery tickets for unlimited hours to make limited money. Meanwhile, I kept switching from one petty job to another, delivering pizzas, stocking shelves at grocery stores, warehouses—stuff like that.'

There was a new intensity marking his face, deepening his tone.

'In all those years, I had one target: to earn money, as much as I could, to give myself and my family the best possible life. I started a security agency and hired young boys, especially immigrants, from the Middle East and Asia. They were ready to work for low wages, provided I could guarantee them the stability of a job.' He leaned back and gazed up at the sky. 'That company grew, and conditions improved with time. Then a friend of mine introduced me to the stock market and cryptocurrencies. I poured my earnings into venture capital.'

'And then…?' she asked, fascinated.

'If time is money and cryptocurrency an opportunity, thankfully, some millennials had both to spare at the right moment. Who would've thought some stocks could expand by 400 per cent? We bought a house in the suburbs of Detroit, and I began an investment firm with my acquaintances from New York. Not much later I bought a house in Nashville, then one in Petersburg, then Orlando, and then closed a few condominium deals in Vegas.'

Meera smiled wryly. 'All these houses and you still care to see your village home?'

'When my grandfather passed away in the village and my uncles took over his land, that house was all they'd left to my father. I wanted to see it.'

She gazed at his overwhelmed face. He looked down and sniffled, his eyes glassy with tears. Then suddenly, he grinned, throwing back his head. She watched him wordlessly for several minutes till he was peaceful at last.

'You're hungry?' she asked.

He ran his fingers through his hair and touched the back of his head while gazing at Meera. 'A little bit.'

'I know a place you'd like,' she said and opened the door to the driver's seat.

∞

At a restaurant in the bustling Khan Market, neighbouring India Gate, Aniket pondered over the menu before placing an order. Meanwhile, Meera continued to wonder if Aniket's story had touched or burned her heart—she was sure, at least, that it had done something. No one had ever imagined Aniket would go on to do something impressive. He'd been a selfish child, below average in academics and unreliable when it came to friendships. At arts, music, and extracurricular activities, Meera had always outpaced both Sunny and Aniket. Not a single school-day had their luck ever been so marvellous as to save them from punishments and scolding. Incomplete homework, tattered notebooks, shabby uniforms and rough hair—these traits defined the Aniket she'd known. That said, she remembered his vitality, his tendency to lead too; whether it was while breaking a neighbour's window or climbing up the orchard trees, he had always led them.

A cold storm passed over her body and nipped her soul. *Everyone except me is clear about what they want*, she thought. *Dad wants me to marry into this rich family. Aniket probably wants to marry a decent girl. Mom wants what dad wants and Sunny has a set path to follow.* She shook her feet and looked into the busy kitchen.

'Hope they don't put too much oil. Should I go tell them?' Aniket said, rubbing a tissue over a thin layer of grease on the tabletop.

'You think they'll care about your instruction among the fifty other orders they have?' she mocked, and he looked at the hurrying waiters and kitchen staff.

'Never mind,' he said, then cleared his throat and blinked several times. 'So, how many boyfriends have you had?'

She frowned. 'How many girlfriends have you had?'

'Officially, three.'

'And unofficially?'

'I don't remember exactly, but seven to ten, maybe,' he said, his brows furrowing. 'Your turn.'

'None, but I should've had some,' she said, smiling.
'That's a great idea. You can start with me.' He chuckled.
Meera shot him a wicked grin. 'You wish!'

Five

It was an important day at the office. Namita Shah had summoned a meeting, and people were already rushing into the conference room. Sights of this kind were rare; Namita and her sycophants behaved anxiously only once a year or so. Now, they stood close, making conversation and waving their hands in serious gestures.

The conference hall was crammed with employees from the technical department. They sat around the table and talked in low voices. While Meera wondered dimly what they were talking about, she glanced around to locate a familiar face from her department, but could not find any. She retreated to a corner when Akshita suddenly appeared to surprise her.

'Am I in your blind spot, girl?' Akshita said, clearly taking a dig at Meera for the biker's incident.

Meera sprang from her chair to hug her friend. 'I shouldn't have told you!'

'But you couldn't resist,' Akshita said bashfully, keeping her voice low.

Meera nodded towards the assembled workers. 'What's this mess about?'

Akshita made a face. 'Something happened at one of our production units.'

'Saharanpur plant again?'

'Yeah, that one.'

'Come here. I've found us seats!' SP called, having just snuck in through the side door. The girls waved at him and followed.

Namita Shah began her speech with a greeting as everyone settled down. Polite, pleasant, but authoritative—*very on-brand*, Meera thought to herself. Namita began to talk about the breakdown at the Saharanpur plant and then paused, rising from her chair and strolling silently around the room as if reflecting upon something grave. The employees watched her.

'We can't let it happen right before the audit,' she said at last and then turned to her audience. 'We've long tested the waters; it's time to dive in. Factory supervisors, managers, foremen, they all have tales to tell, but while production is halted, we will keep losing business. We'll visit the plant and sort this matter out once and for all.'

'Yes, we should!' a man shouted, and the rest harmonized.

'Okay then, let's go over the details,' Namita said, and picked up a marker to write on the board behind her.

Meera gaped at her. If a rough day like this had struck any other individual, details like clothing might have been skipped, but Namita never compromised. Not when it came to her appetite for fashion. A shining Rolex on her wrist, a leather Burberry handbag, diamond earrings and over-the-top makeup; she carried it all off.

Meera was reminded of how the lady had handled

rumours about her divorce the previous year. While no one knew the real cause, there'd been plenty of theories circulating about who was to blame, from her bland married life to her husband's ostensible affair with an Australian model. Everyone in the office knew about her husband's extravagant activities and the arguments he used to have with Namita, but these factors were ignored in favour of gossip about his affair, which he ratified by marrying the model five weeks after his divorce with Namita was settled in the family court.

But Namita had smilingly dismissed it all.

'So, what do you think about it, Meera?' Namita enquired, as if sensing Meera's lack of concentration. All eyes in the room fell upon the girl at once.

'Ahmm, it's a great idea,' Meera fumbled, but the lady remained in the same stance, an eyebrow arched.

'So, you would like to join us?' Namita said, nodding to Meera, and two of her sycophants giggled.

Meera nodded, twisting her fingers to cut short the awkwardness.

Akshita kicked her leg under the table.

'Good,' Namita said, clicking her tongue and turning away to face the whiteboard.

'What's wrong, *huh?*' Akshita whispered to her. 'None of us are going to that stupid factory you agreed to go to.'

'Shush,' Meera whispered, lines forming on her forehead. If she was going to join Namita at the factory, she'd need to start paying attention.

Late that evening at home, Meera took a sip of coffee and watched the lights on the road below shift and flicker as the traffic wound its way north. In the distance, two faint lights brightened the sky—a plane gliding towards the runway. The peanut vendor on the corner of the street was packing his wares into a tattered jute sack. The lantern on his cart dimmed as he pushed his cart homeward.

A light breeze ruffled her hair and Meera drew her shawl firmly around her shoulders.

Aniket appeared on the balcony behind her. 'Hey, I've got something for you.'

She glanced up at him. 'What?'

'Promise you won't kick me down this balcony after seeing it,' he said, eyes glinting.

'What is it?' She giggled.

He pulled out a tarnished metal object from his pocket and held it out to her. She ogled it, thoroughly confused. *An old rusty metal? What's this crap?* Then she recognized it: the piece of her bicycle that Aniket and her brother had broken off some twenty years ago.

She screamed and snatched the bell from his hand. 'Where did you find this?'

'In my garage,' he said, laughing.

'I can't believe it! I sobbed about this for almost two days.'

'I'm sorry. You can beat me up now.'

She said nothing for a moment, instead peered into Aniket's smiling eyes. 'Thank you,' she said at last.

He looked away, lights from the road below glittering in his faraway eyes. 'I miss those days,' he said softly. 'The most beautiful, hassle-free, calm…'

She stared at him. She *needed* to say something, she knew, but what? The moment passed. Aniket's eyes were fixed on the distant moon. She sipped her coffee and looked away.

∞

One who doesn't leap at an opportunity when it comes has no right to complain later, Mr Sharma thought to himself, turning the page of the newspaper in front of him. He stared at his daughter, who stood at a safe distance from Aniket. Mr Sharma had practised the art of isolating opportunities from an ocean of risks and wanted his children to learn to do it as well, but Meera was daft. Aniket, Mr Sharma knew, had spent the whole week trying to impress his daughter, but still she acted oblivious to her surroundings. Somehow, Mr Sharma had arranged for the two of them to have dinner on Wednesday and go shopping at a high street mall in South Delhi on Thursday. When he felt sure that Meera would never invite Aniket to her friend's ceremony this weekend, Mr Sharma extended the invitation to Aniket himself. As a matter of fact, he had decided to wait for two or three days more, and if his daughter still didn't understand what she ought to do, then it would be Mr Sharma's affair. He'd have a word with Aniket's father and get the wheels rolling himself.

For her part, Mrs Sharma wondered whether her daughter had lost interest in marriage altogether after spending too much time around her rigid father. She should have been sent away to a hostel or a boarding school for a few years, and perhaps that way she'd have been more social and worldly, Mrs Sharma thought.

Aniket still hadn't gotten a hotel room; Mr Sharma wanted him to stay with the family. The ambience at home was different with him around. All bickering parties were on the same side for once and were trying to get their act together. Breakfast, lunch, dinner, decor, tidiness and even the way they talked to one another—everything seemed groomed. They even wished 'good morning' and 'good night' to each other these days.

Sunny too, was glad. He had his old friend around again; the two of them had been like an iron and a magnet back in the days and used to follow each other almost everywhere.

Six

Saturday evening at the Sharma household was unexpectedly vibrant—a far cry from the family's usual weekend affairs, during which they'd typically sit on the living room sofa while Mr Sharma flicked from one channel to another on the television, making his family watch shows and movies of his choice. For the evening, Mr and Mrs Sharma were brightly dressed to attend a get-together at a neighbour's, and Sunny was straightening his tie, preparing to accompany Meera and Aniket to SP and Akshita's engagement ceremony.

It was 7 p.m. and the two boys still weren't done getting dressed. Meera knocked at their door one final time and received a by-now-familiar reply from the other side: 'Five minutes!'

'How many more five minutes?' she yelled and wondered what enormous preparations the boys were involved in. After all, they hadn't been willing to join Meera for the ceremony until the afternoon.

Holding the sides of her long flared mesh skirt, she fell on to a couch, baffled, considering the five missed calls she'd received from the would-be bride. Apparently, her hairstylist had ditched her at the last minute and she needed an opinion on the simple curls her makeup artist had come up with. Meera propped her back against the sofa and scrolled through various social media feeds until, after a good twenty-five minutes, the door finally opened.

Sunny walked out, looking uncharacteristically neat and handsome. Behind him was Aniket, in a black tuxedo that accentuated his polished looks, yet made him self-conscious; he'd dressed up for many events before but had never been to weddings and engagements as a distant liaison. Meera smiled assuredly at him, and the unease upon his face disappeared under a blush. She then gazed at Sunny, briefly revisiting that moment she'd finally felt proud of his striking appearance: the day when he'd worn his uniform for the first time, the metal badge flashing on his chest. Meera smiled contentedly once more, remembering how it had felt when her own concerns had slipped away in the face of her brother's glory.

'Okay, we're late, hurry up,' she said, clapping her hands.

'I'll get the car,' Sunny said, grabbing the keys. 'Meera, you lock the doors and don't toss the keys into a flowerpot or under the carpet. That's the first place where thieves would look for them.' He chuckled and strode out of the room.

Aniket remained beside Meera as she shut the windows and turned off the lights around the house. In the living room, she wrestled with the knob of one window as Aniket rushed to help her.

'What are you, little buddy,' he murmured at the fast-stuck frame.

'Push this pane,' she said, and he thrust hard at the wooden frame while she slid the latch into place. 'Thanks.'

She glanced briefly at his face.

'You're most welcome,' he uttered, eyes flicking over hers.

The black suit and finely curved lapels over his pale shirt appeared sophisticated under the soft light of the living room. She looked into his eyes, trying to recognize the dark brown that had once gleamed with overconfidence.

She closed the last window and ran a final look around the house. 'I've reminded Sunny multiple times to bring a handyman for these warped windows, but little does he care,' she said lamely, grabbing keys to lock the house.

Aniket spoke hesitantly. 'Ah, uhm, I was saying that…I forgot, my stupid mind!'

'Say it when you remember.' She turned to exit.

'I've remembered,' he exclaimed, gently holding her hand. 'I wanted to say that…I've been watching you for a week… and I'm not complaining, but it seems like you don't belong to any of us.'

She shuddered as a beam of light from the hallway touched her chest.

He looked intently at her. 'Remember how you were the only girl in class I used to act stupid with? It wasn't because I didn't like you, no—it's true that you and I, we're very different. You always looked down on me when, in reality, I wanted to be your friend and share the attention you got from the teachers. You used to have a spark for creating things and then cherishing those creations; you'd find some kind of delight and passion in everything you did.' He took a step forward. 'And now, watching you after all these years… something has gone wrong. I feel like you need help.'

'Help? As in…?' she said, releasing her hand from his grip.

He shifted his gaze to the floor. 'If you don't like me, I'll get out of your hair, but I can't see you mad and low.'

'I'm not mad at you…or anything,' she said.

'This isn't normal. They tell you to sleep—and you sleep; they tell you to eat, and you eat, whether or not you're hungry.'

Meera spoke grimly. 'Maybe you've forgotten, but let me remind you. Girls change when they grow up in this part of the world. I live with my parents; how do you expect me to behave?'

'Stupid of me, I shouldn't have brought this up. But come on, Meera. We can talk. People accept help when they need it. I've been to a counsellor in the US and so have some of my friends. When you get stuck or encounter something that limits your potential, you need to sort it out, that's all.'

'You don't understand boundaries, do you?' she said, her throat damp and eyes wide with humiliation.

He ogled her wordlessly, static and stupefied, as if he was staring at a ghost. Then, he moved ahead and held her face in his palms.

'I didn't mean to hurt you,' he said.

She leaned against the side of the door and looked into his eyes. His fingers ran down her neck slowly. She protested weakly, knowing all the while that her surrender was inevitable. He moved to hold her gently. The frail pieces of her outfit were a hurdle, but his fingers nimbly moved towards her bare waist.

She shut her eyes; her lungs filled with his perfume. She'd never known her body could respond this way; a rush of blood, a sudden and honest outbreak of the senses. She hung on to his arms as he leaned in to kiss her.

She let her hands fall from his chest, but he looked at her, his dark brown eyes gleaming with confidence.

'Go back,' she said, tripping upon the uneven floor.

'I'm not going anywhere this time,' he said, holding on to her torso.

What had been left of her determination vanished, and like a snowflake, she melted against his warm chest again. He took control and pulled her head towards his, kissing her again. This time, though, it filled her mind: the self-esteem he had pricked at while knowing nothing about her. At once, her passivity slipped away. She surged forward, pushed him against the wall, his hands still measuring every inch of her bare body above the sequin-embellished dress.

Perhaps he wasn't completely wrong, she thought, stuck to his chest.

Tears welled in her eyes. Breathlessly, she waited for him to see, to recognize the damage, but it took him a full minute to register that she was inert, and not in the way she'd wanted.

He pulled away, and looking at her face, navigated the dejected mood.

'It is okay. We're friends. You don't have to pretend here.' He spoke smoothly.

She stared back, her mind screaming. Faking calm, she walked away.

Seven

Black and ice-blue. Perhaps the contrast was compelling, or perhaps it was just Aniket Saxena who caused every eye in SP and Akshita's engagement ceremony to turn and look at the three of them. As far as Meera could tell, Aniket had moved past the earlier unpleasantness and had chosen to focus on the good parts only. He seemed different with her now, and she could feel the change; he was more considerate and tender. The persistent smile on his lips and his outward affection suggesting that he was happy to show her off. And indeed, attention was arriving in droves—from everyone.

Even Sunny had caught a whiff of the dish being cooked around him.

Namita Shah was there, surrounded by her constant group of companions, looking as ravishing and splendid as her distinctive reputation would suggest. White pearls around her neck had been elegantly paired with a subtle off-white designer saree. She glanced at Aniket and leaned to the girl on her right, whispering something in her ear.

Meera looked at the flowers outlining the barbicans and the ivory net that loosely hung over the entire lawn. Tree trunks, branches, shrubberies—all were decorated with strings of lights. These were signs of Akshita's input, Meera knew; the food and drinks, however, screamed SP.

Sunny and Aniket walked towards a corner of the lawn, evidently preferring isolation. They found an empty table and sat down together. Within minutes, they had covered the surface of table with kebabs, beer and a portion of chicken breast.

'Hashtag vegan Hindus!' Meera exclaimed, pretending to post a story with her cell phone.

Sunny's smile faltered for a second as he raised the dripping chunk of meat higher. 'Go ahead, I'm not scared,' he said.

A group of colleagues smiled at Meera, and she rose, clicking her tongue. 'I'll save it for some other day,' she said, making a face and headed away to meet her friends.

When she came back some ten minutes later, Aniket was scrolling down the screen of his cell phone while sipping beer. Sunny was still focused on the kebabs, relishing every bite.

Meera frowned. 'If you keep eating at this rate, I'm not bringing you to any party in the future.'

'Let him eat. It's good for his bruised heart,' Aniket said, smiling viciously. He flattened a small yellow slip on the table surface. 'He smiled at a random girl, and she tossed her phone number over to me.'

'Thanks for shooting down my game, brother,' Sunny whined.

Meera narrowed her eyes at the slip. Sunny grinned. 'I can smell the jealousy.'

'Smell your food,' she grunted, but the boys were looking

past her, over her shoulder.

A polite feminine voice rung out behind Meera. 'You mind if I join you guys?'

Meera spun around to find Namita Shah, with two sidekicks behind her. She was as graceful as ever, with a smile as her left hand gently held the back of Meera's chair.

'Good evening, ma'am,' Meera said, rising from her seat at once.

Namita's tone was sophisticated and formal. 'Very good evening, dear. You look gorgeous, I must say.'

'Thank you!'

Namita's extra-long smile wavered slightly. Perhaps she'd expected an identical compliment, but the girl had tripped up, overcome by her boss's sudden appearance.

'Hope you are having a good time here,' Namita said, uncharacteristically humble. Then, pointing her wineglass towards Aniket, she enquired, 'And this young man is...?'

'Oh, I forgot,' Meera said. 'He's a friend from New York. Aniket.'

Aniket kissed Namita's hand courteously and her superficial smile returned.

'If my sources are not wrong, you've got an eye for good stock,' Namita said.

Aniket blushed. 'I just tend to look close and read patterns.'

'And the rest is *magic*.' Namita chucked artificially.

Sunny watched them like an owl—he didn't move or say anything—still holding a piece of meat in his hand. He wasn't mesmerized by her elegance, Meera knew; his reticence was due to a grudge he was holding on to after Namita had overlooked his request on LinkedIn some six months prior. His profile, which only boasted a few connections, wasn't noticed by Namita until he'd added Aniket Saxena to his social circle recently.

'What a coincidence! Just this morning I spoke to my financial advisor about investments and here I am, meeting a Wall Street ace the same evening,' Namita said, her hands carving precise curves in the air, her neck perfectly straight.

'Ah, I'm more fortunate to meet you,' Aniket countered. 'Meera told me a lot about you. Your achievements are commendable.'

'Commendable is your trick. You can buy a racehorse for an apple and an egg.'

Namita was already at it again, her big mascara-lined eyes fixed on Aniket.

'If you'll allow it, I'd like to invite Meera and you over to my house for tea,' Namita said, glancing at Meera with a confidence she had never seen before.

Sunny coughed—a disapproving signal meant for Aniket—but it went ignored. Money, Aniket knew, played above grudges and dislikes.

'So does she complain about her boss?' Namita said, winking at Meera.

Aniket grinned. 'Not at all. I'd bet she's the nicest employee to have around.'

'Undoubtedly. But she's seemed lost for the last couple of days. What have you done to my girl?' Namita smiled, turning partly towards Meera.

Sunny gulped his drink bitterly.

'Rather, she's done something to me,' Aniket muttered,

suddenly reaching for Meera's hand.

Meera looked uneasily around, trying to intercept the glances directed towards her. Namita and her sidekicks smiled, taking sips from their drinks, evidently thrilled to have new material to gossip about.

'So,' Meera said, clearing her throat, 'we're all set for the factory visit?'

'Yes, absolutely,' Namita said.

Aniket looked surprised. 'What factory visit?'

One of Namita's assistants stepped forward—a young woman with large, smiling eyes. 'Something came up at our Saharanpur plant. We're leaving early the day after tomorrow so we can be back in Delhi by evening.'

'All of you?' Aniket asked, directing at Meera, but Namita took it upon herself to offer a response. 'I want to go see myself. My fifty steps would be similar to my staff's hundred,' Namita added, looking briefly at Sunny.

'I see. Wish you all good luck then,' Aniket said.

'So, this Wednesday evening works for you?' Namita asked, smiling again.

'Wednesday for tea—yeah, sure, we'll be there.' Aniket reached out and shook Namita's hand.

Eight

Monday, 5.40 a.m. Meera blinked at the bright screen of her phone before putting it away and peering up at the front gate of her office. She was early and having reached before everyone else, toasted herself silently. There was a dull clanking sound, and the guard pushed open the gate for her.

She'd ironed her clothes last night to save herself the morning rush, but there was nothing for breakfast. Mr Sharma had been up for his yoga session, but she did not want to ask for his help. Wordlessly, as the two usually were with one another, he'd glanced at his daughter—her crisp white shirt, perfectly straight hair and decent-sized heels—and walked her to the door. On top of that, Aniket had been behaving strangely. He desperately wanted her to call off the factory tour, going so far as to spout a list of excuses to get her off the hook without damaging her relationship with Namita, but Meera saw no sense in diverting from the decided track at the last minute. This erratic stuff had never been in her nature.

Dark and cold, there was an edge to the morning, a ruthless pull that kept everyone who had a choice still in bed. Meera steered Sunny's car down into the basement parking lot, two hatchbacks following after her. The engines of the three vehicles turned off almost at the same time.

Meera gathered her laptop from the back seat and suddenly realized that she was missing the housekeys. She cursed inwardly, scanning the passenger seat, but there was nothing to be seen.

Rohan, a colleague of Meera's, emerged from one of the cars and waved to her before running a final check on the lapels of his coat. A woman came out of another car and Rohan wished her good morning. The woman smiled and walked to the elevator without any interest in Rohan's company. Rohan smiled awkwardly and walked towards Meera, who was still hunting for her housekeys in the glovebox of her car, only to come across a pack of condoms. 'Extra dotted, performance-enhancing,' the blue cover read. She slammed the latch of the compartment hard, her face ashen, all sluggishness gone. *Stupid Sunny. Who leaves such stuff in the car before lending the keys to their sister?* She cursed and stepped out.

∞

The office was on the upper floors of the building, but Rohan and Meera chose to kill some time in the hallway of the first floor. A lady from the parking lot had followed the two clueless workers and joined them in the waiting area. Sitting in one of the iron chairs of the reception gallery, Meera had her eyes fixed on her cell phone—clearly, she was unwilling to talk.

The building was as cold as the world outside. Meera curled up in her icy chair and gaped at the long walkway to her left. It seemed to wear a shroud of silence; the pod lights above gleaming coyly on the polished tiles. She tore her eyes away from the view; there was something unsettling about seeing the normally busy corridor so quiet. Between the view and Rohan's inane chitchat, she chose Rohan.

After a moment of expectant silence, Meera realized that Rohan was only curious to learn about SP's ceremony. She gave him few updates and he listened keenly. But, finding no exciting gossip in it, he decided to switch conversation partners. *Good for you*, Meera thought to herself. She picked up her phone and caught a glimpse of her swollen eyes in the front camera.

As the arms of the clock made a perfect vertical line for 6 a.m., more people showed up, shattering the silence of the corridors. Handbags, travel mugs, jackets and stoles filled the iron chairs as people swarmed in, chatting with one another. Some rushed for a cup of coffee while some preferred cigarettes, all of them trying to stir their senses in the cold, misty morning. By quarter past six, more commuters had arrived, filling the last remaining chairs.

'Who chose this hallway to sit in in the first place?' one older employee moaned as she pushed an unattended bag from a chair to the floor. Meera smirked to herself; she'd chosen the location.

Namita Shah's minions arrived a few minutes later. *Funny*, Meera thought, *how they'd been the ones nagging everyone to arrive on time.*

Meera rubbed her neck, but the back of her head still felt heavy. She walked to the coffee booth, hoping an espresso shot would soothe her. Out of the window, a thick layer of mist hung above the concrete, ribbons of sunlight struggling to break through. Meera watched a family of pigeons shuffling their feathers from their position on a telephone cable.

A glossy black Audi made its way through the gate and came to a stop at the entrance of the building just as Meera took a whiff of her espresso. Namita Shah stepped out in a high-collared black jacket and Randolph glasses with a silver frame. She took slow steps towards the building, exuding money and power, and her chauffeur closed the door behind her.

'Good morning, guys,' she said when she emerged a couple of minutes later.

A chorus of greetings swelled in response as employees began to gather around.

'First of all, I want to thank all of you for making it here this morning,' she said. 'If anyone's still behind time or stuck somewhere in traffic, tell them to hurry up as we're leaving in ten minutes.'

She reset her glasses, thoroughly checking all the present faces. 'It's an important day for us and I want you all to pour in your dedication. It will be a long day too, but we'll make sure we accomplish our goals and get back here on time. The bus should be here soon, and you can start boarding as soon as it arrives. Any questions, guys?'

Apparently, there were no questions.

'So, we're good?'

An affirmative murmur echoed across the corridor. Meanwhile, the bus pulled up outside, and everyone started picking up their belongings, filling water bottles, rushing for another round of tea or coffee, hurrying to restrooms or lighting the last cigarettes. Meera knew Namita was right; it certainly would be a long day.

Nine

Roughly 170 kilometres from New Delhi, in northern Uttar Pradesh, lay the district of Saharanpur. It had no tourist attractions or urbanity to its credit, but for a businesswoman like Namita, it had financial pull. The factory there was the company's second-biggest textile manufacturing hub, but for the past five years its performance had been steadily declining. The company had tried to shift their loyalties to other units, but those couldn't come close to meeting the demand.

The issue of minimum wage had once again become central to the problem of conflicts between the management and the workforce. Suppliers, vendors and creditors, the business had been affected at all levels. Moreover, there were reports of problematic machines that had been sitting idle for months without repair.

Namita Shah sighed, wondering how she was going to appease both sides; no matter what, she had to bring the diverse units involved under the terms of the company. It didn't matter to her who had to make the final compromise. She only had to throw promises at them. The fog had grown thicker over the Ghaziabad highway, and the day beyond was white. Mild sunlight peeped through the clouds. *One cannot predict a cold sky, much like a cold heart*, Meera thought suddenly, staring into the cold face of Namita Shah, who was sitting passively next to her.

Out of curiosity, Namita had asked Meera to ride with her in her Audi, and the girl couldn't credit any reason—except Aniket Saxena. The offer had surprised Meera almost as much as it had jolted Namita's sidekicks; they'd stormed into the bus, ogling Meera through the dirty windows, looking as if they'd been stabbed in the chest.

Meera glanced into the rear mirror, spotting the office bus chasing their car down the highway. She imagined how relaxing it might have been to be in it; here, she counted each minute of awkward silence. It hadn't initially seemed bad, especially considering the dark leather interior of Namita's car and the tarnished wood detailing on the dashboard and doors. The girl looked down at her boss's expensive shoes and dragged her modest pair of heels closer to herself, managing to get them under her knees, only out of her sight and not Namita's.

Of course, she received a huge chunk of her husband's wealth in alimony. How else would she own such heaven in her forties? Meera reasoned with herself. *I wonder if she has forgiven the betrayal.*

'Can you pass me that bag?' Namita said, breaking the silence and pointing at a handbag lying in the front seat.

Meera leaned forward to lift the leather bag. It was unusually heavy.

'It's got weight,' Meera uttered as Namita caught hold of the straps.

'I like to keep my gun in there.'

Meera stopped herself from gasping. 'I see,' she managed.

'I bought it last year. Staying alone, you know...it's scary sometimes.' Namita shrugged.

Meera mumbled, 'How does it feel? A house with so many rooms and just one dweller...' As she spoke, her shoulders drew together, and her torso pulled back slightly; she'd asked what no one at work had probably dared to ask Namita before.

The lady quivered, and Meera felt the atmosphere shift, the air turning heavy and ambiguous.

'There has always been one dweller there—me,' Namita said curtly.

A dozen more questions floated inside Meera's head, but lacking the nerve to speak, she lapsed back into silence and stared at her phone. Then, finding her social media feeds dull, she turned away and peered outside. Namita certainly wasn't just anybody's cup of tea—*Not mine at least*, she thought. A hundred Meera Sharmas working together would not be able to comprehend one Namita Shah, because people like her lived more than one life, depending on where they were, who they were with, and what they wanted from that person. And, between all those lives, there were perfect partitions, each distinct personality strictly confined to its section.

'So, you're good with Aniket?' Namita said, not looking up from the documents she was skimming through.

Meera shrugged. 'Yes.'

'Nice. Looking forward to marrying him?'

'Not at the moment, but yes, some day,' Meera said. She wanted to tell the truth, to explain the real situation with

Aniket, but she didn't want to lose the respect she'd only recently started receiving.

'Take your time, it is a big decision. Doesn't matter if things are all gold-plated on the surface.' Namita smiled.

'Sure,' Meera said as she looked into Namita's eyes.

For the first time that morning, Meera was able to look closely at her face—the eyes smoked black to the edges, shifty and dominating. Meera blinked several times, shifting her view as the lady went back to reading the documents.

'This is confusing.' Namita sighed, and Meera didn't know whether the woman was talking about the papers or Aniket. Her voice stayed low; she wasn't the quiet type at the office, but now she looked tense, even sad. Meera wanted to say something, but let her thoughts go, deciding to focus on her first-ever luxurious ride.

The highway was broad and smooth. The road was lined with rows of eucalyptus trees, scrubs and wild grass, while the land beyond the highway was covered with crops. Small shanties and restaurants faded along the road and Meera imagined the peace naturally prevalent there, where people worked with little pressure and fewer expectations. Cattle in thatched barns and roaming in barren lands appeared as the car moved deeper into the northern state, and she fantasized about the simple lives of its inhabitants. Her village in Dehradun was like these deprived settlements and she'd loved it just the way it was. Subconsciously, she wanted to pull over at one of the highway restaurants—not for the food, but for sunshine and tranquillity.

Three and a half hours later, the outside world began to change. Road directions appeared, pointing towards

Saharanpur, which seemed dark beneath the shadow of the huge factory in the city's suburbs. Namita's chauffeur steered down a bypass, which was not smooth like the highway they'd just left. The brick lane was rather old and dusty. Fine powder covered the black Audi, caking the windscreen. A slight line of disgust rose upon Namita's forehead as the tyres of the car shuddered upon the uneven surface.

'Slow down,' she yelled at the driver. 'Don't you have common sense?'

'Sorry, Madam.'

'You see this, Meera? It's the road to the factory.' She shook her head. 'No wonder these crises are swallowing our company. Everything is chaos here.'

'Indeed,' Meera consented.

∞

The dusty premises clearly signalled to Meera just how boring the factory would be inside. The tour bus passed through the gates of the production unit, following Namita's car towards a group of people waiting to welcome them. Some management-level men were wearing suits and kept their hands clasped behind their backs, while others were dressed more shabbily. Their smiles could be spotted from a distance. Meera reckoned if these were the same men who were supposedly protesting and making demands. Perhaps the arrival of Namita Shah was enough for them to overlook their frustrations.

Meera stayed beside Namita, carrying her boss's files and handbag. She'd been chosen as Namita's companion for the day, much to the chagrin of Namita's jealous pair of assistants, who shot Meera dark looks from their position at the back of the group.

The foremost man—whom Meera guessed to be the chief supervisor—stepped forward to greet them and tossed a flower garland around Namita's neck. Several other garlands settled around her and a mass of employees encircled her with greetings. Meera jostled left and right, bodies pushing past her, while she tried to keep Namita in sight. Even from here, she could see the look of disgust crossing her boss's face.

∞

Contrary to Meera's expectations, the factory office was rather clean and several indoor plants marked the path towards the meeting room. The meeting room was a sizeable hall, capable of accommodating a group of fifty or so. The room lacked heat, and its location on the outskirts of town was evident; train horns honked somewhere nearby. The floors were of modern laminate, but the walls and windows were in garish styles, torn out from some '80s catalogue. Some photos, black-and-white, from the golden days of the factory were displayed on all sides of the room. Meera saw there was even a portrait of Namita's ex-husband and her late father-in-law. She glanced at Namita, who took a deep breath and blinked as she eyed those walls—clearly, she was offended by these portraits.

The panel of managers settled into chairs on a concrete platform at the front of the room while the others were directed towards red plastic chairs laid out in several rows facing the panel. Meera followed Namita to the centre of the platform and laid the files down on the table. Namita nodded and peered through her spectacles as she skimmed through the papers. The mass of factory workers—most of them villagers, Meera supposed—watched her intently. It was as if they were staring at a particularly interesting zoo animal.

'My brothers and family members, I've no words to tell you how delighted I am to be among you after so long,' Namita began.

'How come her hair's red?' one man in the crowd spoke in an audible whisper to another, eyes fixed on Namita.

'It's dye,' another man said.

Namita twisted her nose, causing lines to appear on her forehead. For once, she seemed to forget her composure, but somehow, she took hold of her anger and spoke. 'I've been hearing your pleas constantly while I've been away and it's saddening to know that we now have so many differences. I, therefore, on behalf of my late father-in-law, who founded this factory and who took great pride in its growth, extend an apology to each one of you.'

Meera looked around the room and found Namita's apology slipping down into the villagers' hearts already. A train honked outside, rising above the sound of the employees' applause.

'We shall first begin with the spinner problems. I'd like to hear from our foremen, who sweat to keep those machines going,' Namita said, and a group of foremen rose, their chests inflated with self-worth.

Soon, teams of technicians were following groups of foremen to different machines while Namita sat, surrounded by managers and production charts, all enmity forgotten.

Ten

Meera's phone must have shuddered with calls some seven times during the discussions. Five of those missed calls were from Aniket, while the remaining two were from her mother. Doubtlessly, she was worried about Meera coming home late. The meeting had stretched beyond the allotted five hours and an extra two hours had been wasted on looms and colour machines. Replacements had never been on the agenda, but Namita promised that quality repairs would begin within the next month while the team took sample pictures and prepared a thorough report.

It was 7.30 p.m. and the sky had become grey. A low fog had begun to thicken in the cool air—perhaps due to the wide-open terrain and irrigation at nearby mustard fields. There was a crispness to the rural wind. Rohan stood close to the bus, smoking a cigarette; the smoke mingled with the scent of freshly watered soil. He was tired like the others; he too did not expect the meeting to take this long. There had been two refreshment breaks so far, but discussions had stretched for long and grown repetitive, adding to the sense of unpleasantness brought on by the pungent smell of bleach and dye that permeated the entire factory.

Bus riders began to settle into their seats while Meera waited on her boss, who was finishing some paperwork. In desperate need of air, Meera walked out into the courtyard and discovered one of her teammates vomiting. She held her hair, feeling grateful that she hadn't had to endure the factory's repugnant odours since she had stayed with Namita in the office for the most part of the day.

'Everything good?' Rohan asked her as the woman continued to throw up.

'Doesn't look good to me,' Meera said, patting the back of the sick woman.

Namita arrived upon the scene, and sighed at once. 'Oh god.'

'Should we call for medical aid?' Meera asked Namita.

'What aid can we expect from a bunch of rustics?' Namita said, her eyes flashing with annoyance. 'Come on, be strong. You can do this.' She patted the back of the sick employee and helped her stand.

Meera ducked under the woman's other arm and together they helped her towards the bus. With this done, Namita said a final goodbye to the local group who had assembled in the courtyard to see her off. Several important members of the group pushed ahead to bid Namita farewell in person, while their subordinates stood behind, smiling respectfully. With a final wave, Namita slid inside her Audi, which shone fabulously black once again.

Meera climbed in beside her and with a curt nod from Namita, the chauffeur pulled away.

As soon as they crossed the factory's gates, Namita heaved

a sigh—her eyes shut, shoulders dropped loose and back relaxed in the seat. The car rolled down the coarse brick road towards the highway.

'You remember Wednesday's appointment?' Namita spoke slowly, coming out of her motionless stupor a few minutes later.

'Sure, I remember,' Meera said gently.

'When is Aniket flying back?'

'Friday night.'

'I see… We can bring the meeting forward if you'd like. Tomorrow evening?' Namita said.

'I'll speak to him.' Meera suppressed a smile, feeling a bit tickled; none of her colleagues had ever been to Namita Shah's bungalow.

Namita looked away. Her voice was gentle when she spoke. 'Your dad and my husband used to be good friends. Pool, squash, tennis…Ajeet loved playing it all, and your dad was good company. Things change so quickly. We just need to be patient enough to recognize the moment when it comes.' Namita's mouth was a steady line, giving nothing away.

Meera looked at her, surprised by her informal tone. She didn't know how she should respond—formally, informally, sympathetically, or if she should just act ignorant. Realizing she had been silent for too long, she settled on the last option, hoping to avoid complicating things further.

The driver went slowly, evidently distrustful of the dust and uneven road. He didn't want to hear about his lack of common sense again. Namita leaned back against the headrest of her seat and closed her eyes. The chauffeur, thinking he'd gain back some points, put on Namita's favourite playlist of

'80s hits.

'Turn down the volume! Don't you have any common sense? My head is hurting!' Namita screamed.

'Sorry, Madam,' the poor man uttered and hastily turned down the volume.

'He's been working for me for twelve years and acts like he was hired yesterday!' Namita groaned.

Meera held her breath. 'Twelve years, that's a long time,' she said and peeped at the man, who didn't falter a bit. Instead, he wore a content smile on his face.

'Yes, Madam. My father worked at Madam's bungalow and my elder brother took care of her lawns for many years,' the man said proudly. 'The only thing that Madam demands is honesty, and she'd never pull back her hand at anything. She paid for my daughter's school and her marriage. She has a heart of gold.' He glanced back at Meera in the rear-view mirror. 'I'll show you my daughter's wedding pictures when we get back.'

Namita looked at him and he fell silent. Picking up her handbag, she rummaged for something inside—a tiny case of pills—and placed one under her tongue. Then, she shut her eyes and let her head sink back. She remained like that for about three minutes.

'Meera, let me tell you something: no matter how genuine you think someone may be, never trust them blindly. We humans make mistakes all the time. But there are levels of mistakes.'

'Water?' Meera asked nervously, extending a water bottle towards her boss.

'I don't need it,' Namita said, reading Meera's unease.

'So I was saying…there are levels of mistakes.'

Meera ogled her boss as if hearing a dead woman talk. Her mind was full of doubts, both about the pill and the lady herself—she'd never imagined Namita would have a vulnerable side. The chauffeur kept driving down the uneven road, calm, as if he was used to this scenario.

'I know what you're thinking,' Namita said evenly. 'Your father knew of my husband's wrong deeds and yet did nothing. I did what I had to for my children, and for this estate. Your father did what he had to—for his friendship. But if you think I hired you because I forgot what he did, you're wrong. I do not forget things. You're here because you're different from him.' She turned towards Meera, who noticed her eyes had a glazed, faraway quality to them. 'It takes commitment, hard work and focus to run a business, which my father-in-law put in for forty years and now, I'm doing the same. These traits, my girl, cannot be simply inherited; one must be willing to learn them.' As she spoke, the skin around her eyes crumpled, pushed inward, and then became motionless.

The car slogged through the loose gravel, and the fog obscured the bus behind them. The only signs of its presence were two dim circles of light—headlights flashing, as if from underwater. Cane fields ran alternate to mustard saplings along the sides of the road, eventually giving way to barley. Their shadows formed slowly shifting patterns that swelled and faded as the car passed.

At 8.30 p.m., Meera checked her maps, which suggested that the exasperating part of the journey was about to come to an end. Soon, they'd be on the Upper Ganga Canal route towards Delhi. Namita was dozing in her seat. The stereo volume was set to a minimum, but Meera could still hear the lyrics of an '80s hit by Jagjit Singh— *'How is it that you're smiling so much? What sorrow are you hiding? Destiny is a game of palm lines, and you're just losing by (believing in) those palm lines?'*

Meera felt slothful, her feet aching more than her body, and she stretched her back and slackened her frame.

The brakes of the car slammed tight and both women jerked awake.

'What happened?' Namita shot, squinting through the darkness at a row of rocks lined horizontally across the road. She read the pattern—this was a straight line of obstruction, which could only result after a human intervention, but she managed to tell the driver, 'Must've fallen off a truck. Go out and clear them.'

Meera glanced cynically at Namita. 'But this road is used by our trucks to carry textiles,' she said.

The driver began, still pinned to his seat, 'Madam, I heard some things from villagers, this area is operated by goons. What if...' He peered out in all directions, watching for any sort of movement around the vehicle.

The thought of an ambush at once crossed their minds like a thunderstorm. They looked askance at each other, frozen as if in ice, visually engaged with everything around them, yet comprehending nothing.

They felt the need to speak; if any of them would say something, the fear would dissipate, or at least they could think of something logical. But the silence was long, their eyes talking far more than what they would've said to each other, had they been expressing themselves verbally. After a minute of stillness, they took a breath, somewhat convinced that this sight was only upsetting because they were in a dark, unfamiliar place. Of course, monstrous anomalies surfaced in their subconscious during the passing minute, sights of cruelty, ignorance and debauchery—but these no longer exist in human civilization, they thought. Namita snapped, her eyes still wide open, 'Don't talk like those naïve villagers. It's only natural to find rocks in the wastelands. Perhaps it's a gutless act of one of those protesters.'

The tour bus stopped behind them and its headlights illuminated the dark surroundings at once. Namita pulled out her gun from her bag, partly believing what the driver had said earlier. Seeing that pushed Meera into a vortex of fear, a painful feeling which was different from a headache, but felt almost the same. Her face turned pale.

'Don't worry. Go. I'm here if something happens,' Namita said, and the chauffeur stared at her in the rear view. She pushed the safety latch of her revolver while her hands wrapped firmly around the grip.

'Go now, will you?' she yelled.

The driver stepped out and walked carefully ahead. Meera watched him pass between the beams of the headlights, squinting, looking back and forth across the cane fields on both sides of the road. Namita sat taut, watching. There was a sudden ring, and Meera jumped. Namita, muttering under her breath, glanced at her phone. Rohan. Namita declined the call. A moment later, it rang again, and she gestured for Meera to pick up. But it was too late; Rohan was already off the bus, heading towards the line of rocks, perhaps to help the driver.

'Go back, go back!' Namita hissed to herself.

Behind the two men, dark figures began appearing in the cane field. *Men*, Meera realized with a start, several of them. *All of them held rifles.*

A cloud of dust concealed the scene momentarily, and Meera heard Rohan scream. When the mist faded, Rohan was on the ground, holding his head. One man stood behind the driver, who was now on his knees, his hands above his head.

As if they were in an overrated action movie, the two women stared, unable to believe the view, until one of the armed men slammed the thick stock of his rifle against Meera's window. Meera scrambled back, trying in vain to escape, but her senses refused to function.

He struck again, and Namita pointed her gun at him with shaking hands. She pulled the trigger and the bullet zipped through the glass, leaving cracks and a hole in the pane. Meera screamed, her hands clutching her head as smoke from the gunshot filled the car.

The man backed away, eyebrows raised, evidently surprised by the woman's retaliation. Namita aimed again, hands still trembling, a new intensity in her eyes. She roared, the veins in her neck inflating, and fresh sweat broke upon her temple. The man raised his rifle, his eyes intense and ferocious above his scarf, and scrutinized the two women.

Namita eyed him for a long moment, and the revolver slipped from her hands. Meera held her head down, her eyes shut tight.

Another scarfed man appeared outside Namita's door and thumped on the glass.

Namita screamed as he slammed the butt of his rifle

into the pane, the whole car seeming to shudder, the noise unbearable—

And then it was over.

The glass burst free, covering the cowering women, and Namita threw her hands in the air, her eyes flooding with tears. Slowly, she unlocked the door. The man dragged her out and, grabbing her collar, slammed her head against the side of the car. She fell silently to the ground.

The man on Meera's side knocked at the glass with the tip of his barrel, ordering her to unlock it. She lifted her head and looked at him. He knocked again, and she tried to move but found she couldn't. It was as if she was paralysed. He walked around to the other side and leaned in, grabbing her arm and dragging her free from her paralysis. Meera tried to scream, but no sound came out of her mouth.

∞

The dust had somewhat settled. All twenty-six passengers knelt on the ground with their hands hovering above their heads. Any movement whatsoever, whether of bodies, tongues or wits, could mean death. The only voice that prevailed was that of the troop leader—an uneven hoarse tone that came from a man in his fifties, who wore no scarf and held no rifle. His face was wrinkled and his mean and gritty eyes had loose bags that stretched beneath them, covering half of his cheeks. Below the stern line of his mouth hung a long grey beard.

Meera stared down at the unconscious bodies of her colleagues. A stream of blood was leaking from Rohan's nose, down towards his chin. The bruise on his head didn't bleed, but it was already swollen. Namita was quiet. She didn't moan, despite the cut on the side of her head that dripped blood down her neck. The driver sobbed quietly, high-pitched whines escaping occasionally.

Meera was in better shape than these three, but her limbs still were paralysed. She looked at the man with the olive-brown jacket who had pulled her out of the car.

'If you love your life, give everything you have. But if you dare to act smart, I'll rip apart your flesh,' the leader of the group said, waving his hand at Namita. Clearly, he thought her the most likely to act smart.

Three of his men began to walk among the passengers, snatching everything of value upon the bodies of their hostages: jewellery, cash, cell phones, accessories, wallets, and piled them on a piece of stretched cloth. Some petrified hostages handed over everything they had in their pockets: strips of chewing gum, metro cards, paper slips and parking tokens. Meera saw her most recent raksha bandhan gift from Sunny—a silver watch with a shiny dial—tossed on the heap of burgled items.

'Where's the cash?' the captain yelled to one of his men. 'Ask for their debit cards and pins. I want cash. Right now.'

'Let us go, please,' Namita pleaded.

'Silence!' the leader yelled. 'You can't be trusted. Give me a gun.'

He snatched a rifle from one of his men and touched the barrel to Namita's forehead. She shut her eyes, believing the bullet would split open her skull, but he didn't shoot. Instead, he moved it away, let it sway over the entire group, watching the hostages cower and whimper. He laughed, enjoying this game.

'You, come here,' he said, his eyes halting on Meera.

She looked up at him, panic-stricken. He was staring at her.

'Are you deaf? Walk up here.'

Meera glanced at Namita and found her in tears. Then she looked around, expecting more names to be called out from the group or for someone to plead with the men to try to help her, but nothing happened. Meera felt her legs freeze. At once, the air seemed impossibly thick, too dense to inhale. Somehow, she stood, her hands still held above her head as she slowly approached the man.

She stopped in front of him, her tall frame exposed to the harsh headlights of the bus, which bared the curves of her body and exaggerated her vulnerability. She watched the leader's face change—his frustration faded, and he began to smile. His eyebags stretched across his cheeks and the bushy brows on his forehead rose deliberately.

'Good,' he said. Meera's heart pounded in her chest. She stared at him in disbelief.

They began to depart. The captain and his right-hand man, the boy in the olive-brown jacket, walked towards the company's tour bus, leading Meera behind them. The remaining three covered the hostages and picked up the robbed items. The engine of the bus ignited, and the sound of acceleration reverberated through the cold air.

Meera began to scream. Her capture, she realized, was for no other reason than to appease the captain's sick lust. She slumped to the ground, her breath choked with her own tears, and in that moment, she forgot all about the weapons and pushed herself back as the captain tried to drag her on to the bus. He slapped her across the face, and she struggled even harder, biting at his leg with all the strength she had.

He swore and kicked her in the stomach, and two of his men dragged her away.

Something hard hit her on the head, and she slipped at last into unconsciousness.

Eleven

'Look, this one's going to bring good money.'

Meera stirred, the burglar's harsh voice returning her to consciousness. She was on a moving bus, near the middle, her hands and feet knotted with a jute rope. The four burglars were further ahead, clustered around the front seats, next to the driver.

'Don't touch anything,' the leader said. 'These stupid things are of no use. We needed currency. I don't know how Ferihad will react to this.'

The boys lapsed into silence.

Meera turned away, wincing at the pain in her head, and thought of her family. Or, more specifically, the moment when they'd find out that she was gone. *Dad was right. The world is not innocent. I shouldn't have left home. My mom. I wish I could see her one last time.*

'We'll manage something,' said the man in the olive-brown jacket, the first words to pass his lips after almost two hours. 'One problem at a time. This girl, we can't take her along.'

Meera did not move; she kept her eyes closed, pretending to be unconscious.

He walked over to her, and stared at her for a moment, his face expressionless. She froze with fright. He waved his fingers under her nostrils and looked closely at her head.

'Alive,' he said.

'She's a stiff piece. Ferihad will like her,' the leader said, joining the man next to Meera and patting him on the back.

'But, Haza, this wasn't required,' said another boy. 'Those dogs out there will come sniffing for her. Kill her or throw her away; we can't go ahead like this. It'll trigger more risks than the theft would've on its own.'

'Keep your mouth shut, son of a bitch. You shouldn't have boasted of your bravery if you were planning to chicken out every time. Could've stayed at camp, coward. We will disappear from this area before any dog can sniff us out, you get that?'

The boy went tongue-tied. The knife of humiliation jabbed into his chest. He stared at the leader, his fist twitching, and then walked away. Silence prevailed.

Meera knew her bruised head and battered shoulder needed care, but she couldn't worry about that now. There were more pressing questions: *should she try to escape, or should she kill herself?*

One man, separate from the group, came to sit in the opposite seat. His face was covered, and his eyes roved back and forth—from the abducted girl to his teammates.

'Water,' she said weakly to him, propping her head up against the armrest.

He moved upon hearing her plea and pulled a water bottle from one of the back pouches of the seat. She looked at him for a moment before snatching the offered bottle while the other four thugs, as well as the driver, turned towards her. She gulped down the entire bottle and then crashed back into her seat.

'Let me go, please,' she whimpered.

The captain looked at her and sneered. 'Tie her mouth,' he said, and turned away.

∞

Dreams are a vague summary of the past day's feelings, Mrs Sharma told herself, waking up from a nightmare. She'd just seen her little daughter tumbling down a hill beside their old house in Dehradun. She'd run to catch her, but Meera had disappeared first, and then the hill had faded as well.

She opened her eyes and struggled for breath, her lips parched and trembling.

Weird; we haven't visited that house in years.

She got out of bed and hurried to her daughter's room. She knocked on the door. No reply. She entered. The bed was empty. She slid the drapes away from the window and checked the washroom, but there was no sign of her daughter.

Suddenly restless, she turned and marched out of Meera's room, her footsteps thudding through the house. Soon, everyone was awake. Mr Sharma, blinking through his spectacles, scratched his bald head and pressed his hands to his eyes, unable to believe he'd gone to sleep without checking on his daughter. Aniket called her office, firmly clutching the receiver of the landline, but when the conversation was over, the receiver fell limply from his hand.

He gulped the lump that had formed in his throat and

pulled at his hair with shaking hands.

'They took her,' he said weakly.

'Who?' Mr Sharma shouted and snatched the receiver. Mrs Sharma didn't wait to hear any more; she remembered the hill and her falling daughter.

'Mom!' Sunny yelled as she collapsed into his arms.

∞

Eight o'clock in the morning—police vans and ambulances rattled around the small village of Saharanpur. Cops with search dogs combed the area, discovering several shoe prints in the wet soil of the cane fields. Flocks of villagers hurried across the cordoned-off site, scared and curious. The group of released hostages had been moved to the civil hospital, and reports about the most seriously injured two—Namita and Rohan—were positive.

Paparazzi waited keenly at the gates of the hospital for Namita to walk out. Pictures from the crime scene had already bounced business for media houses. Sure, incidents like these weren't new, but the stakes were higher this time, as Shah Industries was in the spotlight.

Namita lay in her hospital bed, her head draped with bandages and soaked in antibiotics. The traumatic sight replayed in her brain every time she tried to close her eyes, so she fixed her gaze on the ceiling. Her staff sat by her side, waiting for her to speak.

∞

The theories devised by Officer Yadav and his subordinate, Rana, regarding the identities of the five muggers were uncountable; old theories overlapped with the new, the web thickening with each new suggestion. It didn't help that none of the local gangs had taken responsibility.

'No, it's impossible,' Nandu said. He was a local gang rat, reeking of alcohol. 'No one has come from outside and broken into our area. I work for Raju and we control the supply of firearms. Not a housefly can escape our eyes. If someone had broken into our area, we would have dealt with him in our way.' The man spat a gobbet of tobacco near the shoe of the police officer.

The policeman stared at him and rose to his feet. He was still for a moment, then threw himself at Nandu, pinning him to the wall behind.

'We need the girl alive,' the officer grunted.

Nandu only chuckled. 'The girl will be dead…or she would have been sold into some whorehouse by now.' Nandu's hand strayed to the locally made gun tucked into his waistband. His eyes were red, opium-misted.

Subordinate Rana gestured for the officer to take his hand off Nandu's collar.

'I'll bring information about the girl, but it'll cost money,' Nandu said, straightening.

Yadav scowled at him. 'And if your information is wrong?'

'Then what? You'll lock me up—like the other seven times?' Nandu said and laughed.

Yadav made a fist and yelled. 'This time I'll make sure you don't get out.'

Subordinate Rana jumped into the situation. 'You'll be

paid. We need a lead as soon as possible.'

Nandu spat on the ground and said, 'Send over the money first.'

The officer and Nandu stared at each other. Finally, Nandu shrugged and turned to leave.

Policemen walked out towards their parked police jeep.

'Keep an eye on these cockroaches, I don't believe them,' the officer grunted to the subordinate.

As he opened the door, Officer Yadav's cell phone rang.

'Sir, we found the bus near the Uttarakhand border, but there're no traces of the girl's body. It's like they've disappeared.'

'Disappeared where? Into thin air?' Yadav spat.

'We're trying, sir.'

Yadav sighed, massaging his temple with his free hand. 'Okay. Keep looking, they can't have gone far.'

Twelve

The evening air smelled of garlic, onions and green chillies. The window of the first-floor room faced a busy street; several vendors and street restaurants served flocks of customers. Meera lay upon an old frayed sofa in the corner of a dark room, the fragrance of milk and carrot pudding cooked with cardamom and nuts filling her nostrils. She tried to distract herself by turning her nose towards the sofa, which smelled only of moisture and worn upholstery. Stronger than everything else, the smell of phenyl rose from the floor, adding a chemical edge to the usual mustiness of a substandard room.

Her head and shoulder felt better today, but her wrists were in pain due to the tight bindings. Even after Haza had told his men to be nice to her, they had not been lenient with her, except allowing her food and restroom use.

She'd seen their bare faces, their light skin tone hinting at north Indian origins and their many scars telling their thuggish histories. Two of them were teenagers—Meera guessed between seventeen and nineteen—while the other two appeared to be in their mid-twenties or early thirties.

Haza's right-hand man, who'd dragged Namita out of her car, didn't speak much. His eyes—light, undaunted and sharp—were ever-watchful, constantly surveying his teammates. He was tall, well-built and implicitly controlled the decisions made in Haza's absence. Meera pretended to be asleep while observing a burn scar on his back; it extended from his neck to his abdomen.

The other man, also tall and masculine, sat by the window, cleaning the bore of his rifle with a piece of cotton flannel. Subtly, he lined the neat parts of the disassembled guns on the table in front of him. He checked upon Meera regularly, and sometimes he spoke to the two teenagers about their work. Meera watched his focused crisp brown eyes from across the table and detected an indifferent, discreet approach from his demeanour. He seemed to have more in common with his weapons than with his fellows.

The two teenagers, meanwhile, were tall, though slimmer than their older comrades. One of them sat close to the gun-cleaning man. His eyes were restless, and made inane comments, lurching for some conversation or pastime. But the man offered nothing more than single-word answers. Periodically, the teen yawned, stretched his body and walked around the room. He looked at the other teenager, as if they had something innate in common.

'Stop staring,' groaned the other teen, catching Meera glowering at him from the corner of the room. She turned away, unable to speak through the thick chunk of cloth that had been stuffed into her mouth.

'She has nowhere else to look,' said the man cleaning the guns.

'Haza has lost his mind with age, picking up trash from everywhere. Swear on my weapon, I'll chop his head off next time he hurls abuse at my mother,' the teen rambled. 'I should have actually done that, at the sword drill in the camp. I'm silent because of you, Sumer bhai, can't you see what he's doing?'

Haza's right-hand man looked at him, his eyes gleaming. The teen swallowed. Perhaps this older man had some connection with Haza that went deeper than a shared job.

'I see everything. You don't need to remind me. Now, I told you to go to the pharmacy. Go before they shut it,' the man—Sumer, Meera remembered—said, and the boy became quiet.

'Can I go with him?' the other teen said, rising.

'Why? Is he picking up a dead body from the pharmacy? Why does he need your help?'

'I want to eat jalebi,' the teen said.

Sumer shook his head. 'Not now.'

The boy sighed and dropped back on the bed while Sumer handed a fifty-rupee note to the other teen, who turned and left the room.

∞

The fact that they've revealed their faces means one of two things, Meera told herself. *Either they don't fear identification because they know I won't see more than a few days, or, as Haza suggested, they're going to give me to some man named Ferihad. Damn, it's all making sense now. I never forget my house keys, but yesterday, I did. It is as if someone in heaven knew I wasn't returning home. My friends wanted me to cancel this tour, but I refused, and this was the first time I'd left Delhi by myself in years.* Tears rolled down her face. She looked out at the partly setting sun and the orange sky that glowed in its wake, covering the horizon of Haridwar city.

She'd never seen death so close, but it felt beautiful, like the setting sun. No hassle, no fights, no explanations—it calmed everything, making her feel fortunate to have lived at all, to have experienced everything she'd once fussed over. Calmly, she accepted her fate, understood that she had perhaps saved twenty-five lives by losing her own. This, she told herself, was the greatest thing she could hope to have achieved in her lifetime. She shut her eyes, feeling weak and accomplished simultaneously.

The door burst open and the teen swaggered back in, a small plastic bag in his hand. He closed the door behind him after glancing out down the corridor.

Sumer glanced up, a cigarette smouldering in his hand, while the other man, Hoque, finished packing the last gun in a big duffel bag. This done, he slid the bag under the bed. The atmosphere was dry and ambiguous. The newly arrived teen walked to the sofa where Meera lay and with clumsy hands, tore the gag out from her mouth.

They weren't going to feed her this time, nor give her water—*they were going to drug her*. Meera screamed. The teenager recoiled, startled, and Sumer rushed to her side and pressed his palm against her mouth, tucking another hand under her head. He glared as she struggled, trying to scream. The other teen turned the television volume up and closed the windows.

'Silent!' Sumer hissed, pushing down upon her mouth.

She stared at him, her veins inflated, eyebrows curved inward. Finally, she quietened. Blood flushed on her face.

'You're not dying so soon, don't worry,' said the teen to Meera. 'We just need to clean your face before we go out in public. We can't stay here for long.'

'Get her water,' Sumer ordered, eyeing the teen, who retreated, head bowed. Then he turned to glare at Meera. 'Don't you get it? Huh?' he hissed. 'I hear your scream one more time, I'll silence you forever. It's better for you if you cooperate.'

Meera stared back at him, her eyes widening.

'Be grateful that we're being nice to you.' He removed his hand from her mouth. 'Give me that disinfectant,' he called to the teen before turning back to Meera.

She sat in silence. The skin around her lips was pale and dry, her eyes swollen, and her cheeks had blackened from tears drenched in eyeliner. A cut—a relic from the previous night—ran from her mouth down to her jawline. Sumer dipped a cotton swab in the disinfectant and dabbed gently at her skin. She frowned as the liquid seeped into the cut. His fingers shook. He blinked and lifted the swab.

'Please don't gag me again. I'll do as you say, I promise,' she said.

Sumer did not reply. Instead, he picked another swab and wiped around her eyes and forehead.

'It chokes me, please. You've got to trust me if you are going to take me out in public,' she said, staring pleadingly at Sumer.

He glanced at her and then at the teen who'd divulged

their plan of going out. The teenager looked down, and then away.

'Okay, but if you try anything smart…'

'I won't, I promise,' she said as he threw away the last cotton swab.

She sat up. The teen handed her a bottle of water and she drank slowly.

Sumer looked at her. 'So, Meera Sharma from Delhi?'

Meera glanced up. 'How do you know?'

'You're all over the news,' said the teen from his place on the bed.

'I told you this would happen,' the other teen said.

'I can't believe we're going to let her walk on the road,' Hoque said.

Sumer took a deep breath, ignoring Hoque's comment. 'Emre, give her new clothes and make sure no marks are on her face,' he said, laying down the disinfectant and glancing down at Meera. 'Girl, go to the washroom and change. We're leaving in half an hour.'

Thirteen

Families, groups of seniors, and gaggles of tourists swarmed the wide streets of Haridwar. Religious booths stretched on both sides of streets leading to the Ganga river, selling shimmering red cloth, rudraksha beads, rosaries, garlands, mythology books and cassettes. Some dealt in brass articles, others in gemstone jewellery, but they all smelled dimly of smouldering incense. Holy songs rang from a dozen DVD players.

Meera had heard many of them before while staying with her grandparents in the village. Her grandmother used to hum them while doing household chores or while watching cattle in the barn. The songs hadn't changed much: the lyrics extolled the goddess Ganga and Lord Shiva alongside the melodies coming from the sitar and the tabla.

Meera was dressed like a hundred other women: her head was covered by a woollen shawl, traditional clothes masked her body and she murmured a prayer. Four men guarded her in four directions, and she followed the two to her front. She behaved as she'd been told: *walk straight, make no eye contact with people approaching from the front, don't pause, and don't even think of being smart.*

From the temple down the bank an aarti began, with the swelling of sacred flames and ringing bells. The roads became crowded as groups started surging towards the temple, but Meera followed her guards against the current across the Ganga. She glanced briefly at the reflections of the flames on the water; the devotees beyond were floating diyas on the flowing river. She took a deep breath.

Her pace slowed as a crowd of devotees walked into her path, and lost track of the two men in front of her.

'Walk fast,' Sumer muttered from behind her.

She shivered and pushed herself through the crowd.

∞

Their new hideout was another musty room, this time on the outskirts of Haridwar. Meera stayed in her corner. *Someone else in my place would've tried their best to escape, come bullet or blade. Opportunities like this are rare, and I wasted it entirely. Still, at least they've not tied my mouth again. Perhaps they trust me now.*

The new room was spacious. Its front faced the highway and mustard fields lined with eucalyptus trees stretched out behind it. The furniture and fixtures were outdated. Modern landscape paintings covered three of the walls and fresh paint hinted at recent renovations, but the pillows and upholstery felt damp.

'Ferihad is stuck. We may have to forget the plan,' Sumer said to the assembled men. He looked tired, Meera thought, and was resting in a chair facing the bed.

'Haza was stupid to count on him in the first place,' Hoque snapped. 'Ferihad is already an irritant in many eyes, especially since the elections. As long as he remains in the city, there will be doubts. Wherever he goes, they follow him. He's of no use to us.'

'Who are we to question their decisions. We have our orders. It has to happen this way,' Sumer said coldly, cutting off one of the teens, who had his mouth open, perhaps to add to Hoque's statement. 'Emre, bring food. Take this money,' he said.

Emre—the silenced teen—rose sulkily and walked to the sink in the washroom. There he splashed water on his face and fixed his hair.

'Get my cigarettes too,' added Sahil, the other teen.

Meera watched Hoque and Sumer looking at one another. The two were clearly in disagreement. Finally, Hoque exhaled, folding the sleeves of his jacket, his eyebrows drawn together, and his lips pressed tight. He rose and, without another word, marched out of the room.

Sumer watched him go as he shuffled a deck of cards. Then, glancing up at Sahil, he dealt the cards and took a long, faltering breath.

'Come, Sahil,' he said at last, 'let's play.'

Meera watched them play, relaxing in their new-found calm. Finally, she cleared her throat. 'Why don't you let me go?' she said. 'I can get you enough money. My father is well off, and my fiancée is rich too. You can ask for any price you desire.'

Sumer and Sahil stared at her, and the older man scoffed.

Meera held her breath.

'Look, girl, we know who you are. To remind you one last time: we don't need your money. Do not ever try to buy us again,' Sumer said.

'Why did you rob the bus then?'

'Aye!' Sahil yelled.

Sumer tossed his cards across the table, his eyes blinking in disbelief.

'Tie her mouth. I've been nice enough to her,' he snapped.

Meera gulped. 'Sorry, I won't speak. I'm sorry.'

But it was too late. Sahil was already on his feet, the gag in his hand.

∞

Later that night, Sumer, Hoque and Sahil headed out for a smoke, leaving Emre behind to watch Meera. He sat across the table, frowning down at a newspaper crossword as an India–England cricket game played on the television. Wind swept over the open fields, rattled the windowpanes and rustled the leaves of the eucalyptus trees. The sound of traffic rose from the highway.

Meera mumbled from under the gag and made a gesture for water. Emre pulled the gag free and held a bottle of water to her lips. She gulped half of it down before pushing the rest away. Then, she threw her head back, feeling her neck twinge and face deficient of blood.

'Give me two minutes please,' she said before he could lean in to gag her again.

'Your name is outshining everything, eh? "Brave daughter, goddess…"' He giggled, flattening the newspaper and reading the subheading out loud. The reddened skin around the acne on his face rose and stretched, his eyes squinting, and an ugly smile widened as he skimmed through the other columns.

Meera watched him—his light facial hair, muted skin tone and brown eyes. It all hinted at an upbringing in the mountains.

'See how using women, children and religion—three all-time classic tactics—can sell anything,' he said and paused. 'Okay, now your time is up, goddess.' He picked up the cloth to tie her mouth.

The skin around her lips and nose stiffened and then grew supple as she looked away. 'Please don't do this. I won't speak, promise.'

'If Sumer bhai finds out, he will kill me. But I can make it a bit looser for you,' Emre said, tying the cloth loosely around her face, enough for her veins to pump blood. His gaze lingered for a moment on the goosebumps coating her arms. Not looking directly at her, he laid a blanket around her shoulders.

'You know, you really shouldn't have made that proposal this morning,' he said. 'You don't know us. It's *good* that you don't. We are not thieves; we don't hunt for money, but for other things. I've known Sumer and Hoque bhai since I had nothing but a mortal body and immortal debts. They settled my debts—not with money, but with bullets. I would've never worked for a shallow man like Haza if Sumer and Hoque bhai hadn't asked me to. Haza knows he can't trust me with his life. We don't lose our pants to women like that pig does.'

Meera listened calmly as the boy spoke. Her gaze held as, word by word, she began to feel increasingly lost in another world, where nothing normal existed and the decree of weaponry was the only rule.

Emre had finished, it seemed. He looked around for the television remote and the two fell back into silence.

Fourteen

Mrs Sharma lay on her bed, the drawn drapes blocking all sunlight, a jug full of water and her blood pressure pills upon the table beside her. Her eyes were dry and swollen, and her face was drained of blood. She stared at the blank wall opposite, her heedless heart beating on, the corners of her mouth twitching. Tears rolled silently from the edges of her eyes. Low on pulse, faith and focus, she questioned at last the Lord she'd worshipped all her life—*Was everything now at an end, all in confusion and breaking into pieces? How would she live in peace if the future held no answer to anything? Is there somebody in heaven at all who could help distinguish between right and wrong?*

Mr Sharma pushed the door open gently. Pushing his spectacles up, he rubbed his eyes and stretched his shoulders before sitting down on the edge of the bed. His head ached; he'd spent the morning on the phone, arguing with the police. He looked at his sobbing wife.

'Why are you crying again?' he enquired softly, dabbing at her tear-stained cheeks with a handkerchief. She shut her eyes, pulling away from him with a jerk.

Mr Sharma looked at her, partly in disbelief. She'd always been a balanced and submissive woman, but losing her daughter had brought out a different side of her. This new woman was unpredictable, blunt and protested against all his decisions. He'd never known such disobedience.

'You knew how shady a woman Namita was, and you sent my kid to work there. She hated us eternally, all of us. She's never been nice to my daughter,' Mrs Sharma yelled. 'Meera wanted to resign. She must've sensed signs of wrong from that witch, but you *failed* to read your child. She was afraid of her. That woman would go to any extent to seek revenge for her broken marriage. It was all her plan, believe me; she wanted to teach us a lesson.'

'Stop it. She had scooped enough money out of that divorce; she doesn't care about hurt feelings any more. And besides, she rode along with Meera, was hurt, got stitches in her head. She's as much in shock as we are. Why would she hurt herself and distort her company's reputation while the entire world is watching her? The media follows her everywhere, she's living a nightmare, just like us,' Mr Sharma said.

'I don't trust that woman or you. I need my kid alive or I will burn that witch. It's all her fault!'

'Okay, calm down,' he said, caressing her forehead.

She jerked away.

'What is it? We're all trying. You can't blame one person for the whole thing.'

'I spent all these years thinking how I was not equal to you. I tried to be like the wives of your friends. Truth is, we can't ever be equal. You lie, you cheat—and that's not even for business, but for your reputation. Now your karma has fallen on all of us.'

He shook his head slowly, scarcely believing what he was hearing. He turned away, eyes bulging, eyebrows lowered.

∞

High above the Aravalli range of hills in western Rajasthan, Sunny piloted a light Cessna aircraft with seven passengers and their luggage towards the Jodhpur civil airport. It was a bright day above the clouds and a thin layer of mist hung in the troposphere. Miles of rocky hills, arid bushes, acacia and prosopis trees punctured the dry terrain stretched out below, and windswept sand dunes rose high as mountains. Where the Thar desert gave way to small settlements around scattered water sources, the thatched roofs of houses, Sunny thought, were tiny dots in an empty country.

Sunny sighed. Flying over water and deserts normally thrilled him, but his eyes and muscles were tired and stiff today. Now, he wished the flight was over already. It was lack of sleep perhaps, or maybe the fact that he hadn't eaten well in two days. He chatted inanely with his co-pilot, trying to prevent images of Meera from flashing before his eyes—sometimes the images ran like a fast-forwarded video, while at other times they slowed down, bringing him snippets of conversations and memories from when they were kids.

He stretched his neck again, shutting his eyes briefly and then flexing them wide. In his head, he battled his own thoughts: *If the history of such crimes is to be believed, his sister is dead. Women are killed after rape in cases where kidnappers make no contact for money or ransom.* His heart froze once again. He was making assumptions, he told himself, overthinking things again. His hand trembled at the yoke. He swallowed the lump in his throat, not willing to give up, not so soon. The nerves around his arm stiffened as he imagined striking the faceless kidnappers, breaking their bones, cutting them and tearing their limbs apart...

The private jet missed its path of descent. The co-pilot glanced at Sunny's face and found sweat pooling on his forehead.

'Glideslope?' he said, his voice taut.

Sunny pushed the yoke forward to control the flight path angle, and the aircraft sloped downward— at a higher altitude than their pre-planned path of descent.

'Cessna five-two-five alpha over the shooting range. Inbound requesting touch and go with information,' Sunny spoke calmly into his radio.

'We're at eighty-five-plus knots with a mile left, and that's before accounting for our deviation from the flight path,' said the co-pilot restlessly.

Sunny didn't reply and continued to reduce the throttle.

'We can't bleed extra speed—and even if we do, it won't be a safe landing,' the co-pilot said. Seeing Sunny firm in his decision, he exhaled sharply. 'We've seven passengers, sir. Let's fly around and come back. Why take the risk?'

'Flying around for five miles because we can't control a tiny situation?' Sunny said. He glanced at his co-pilot, baffled. 'Would you have said the same if we were approaching a high-traffic airport, following a queue of flights? I'm your senior, so listen: things like this happen, and you don't go around every time and waste fuel.'

'Cessna five-two-five alpha, Roger,' came a voice over the radio transmitter.

'Roger,' Sunny said.

The co-pilot stared vaguely at him, as Sunny struggled to bring the plane into glideslope.

'Cessna five-two-five alpha, extend your downwind. I'll call your base,' the air traffic controller said.

'Five-two-five affirmative.'

Although Sunny spoke confidently into the radio, his hands shook as he pushed the yoke forward to move downwind as the landing strip appeared. Then, he pulled down the throttle to maintain power.

'Five-two-five, you can continue straight in. Turn inbound and follow the terminal at midfield,' rumbled the voice on the radio.

The runway was a clear sight. Sunny's breath quickened, coming in and out in rapid gasps. The aircraft entered its path—still too fast.

'Roger, five-two-five. Turning right, following traffic,' he said, while his co-pilot braced for impact.

Sunny's forehead formed wrinkles as he raised his eyebrows. He bit the inside of his lower lip as the flaps of the aircraft extended fully, stalling his speed. He cut off the throttle—the plane bounced. He held back the pressure, keeping the aircraft's nose high, then reduced pressure on the yoke, dumping the extra speed. The aircraft lurched as the wind tore into the extended flaps.

The plane bounced again.

Sunny held his breath; his jaws wedged against each other.

The plane bolted towards the edge of the runway, careening out of control, and he slammed down on the brakes.

Finally, the aircraft achieved taxi speed. Sunny let out his breath, his jaws still locked. He glanced at his co-pilot, who has a brief smile forming on his lips.

Fifteen

Sometimes life does not go as you'd like it to. It may walk plain and subtle for a while, and then, all of a sudden, lose all sensibility and sprint heedless, without a safety latch, oblivious about where it'll land.

Meera compared her fate to a heavenly trial, trying to make sense of her story somehow. '*First of all, I need to find out about these people,*' she told herself. '*If they're not thieves, then who are they? And why have I been tied to a chair for three days if they don't need anything from me?*'

At her kidnappers' third hideout, an isolated place in the north of Haridwar, Meera emerged from the shower in a fresh set of neat clothes, her hair rinsed and wet, the scratches on her face somewhat healed. She sat in her chair and closed her eyes, facing the room's partly open window. Her head felt lighter after having it scrubbed with a shampoo, and her muscles were more relaxed than they'd been in days. Shafts of sunlight fell upon her face, highlighting the pores of her skin, and she ran her fingers gently through her wet hair, trying to straighten a few tangled locks. Her skin, finally released from the dirt, glimmered as if it belonged to some mystic healer, someone able to veil the filth and decay within her beauty. She set the woollen shawl upon her shoulders in a way that would ward off the cold until the next time they released her. Then, moving forward for her wrists to be leashed again, she glanced at the four men, her eyes captivating and eyelashes thick. They ogled her in awe.

Sumer shook his head and forged ahead, binding her wrists. Over and again, he tried to break the spell of alien feelings: magnetism, suffocation and guilt. The girl sighed as the knot pressed against her skin and forced minute lines to appear upon her forehead. He continued gazing. First at her warm eyes, then at her round face and her petite soft nose, symmetrically set between her cheeks. She resembled a woman he'd known a long time ago: his mother, back when she was young and still alive.

Sumer looked away and exhaled before rising. 'Sahil, come with me,' he said. 'Emre, stay here and stay on alert. No TV, no cards and no going out until I return.'

Emre nodded his head.

∞

Moonlight travelled through the closed window of the room, dropping partly on Meera's chair and partly on the floor. The surroundings were soaked in winter's silence—all was still, except for the wind that blew unsteadily from the Shivalik hills to the north, whipping fallen leaves from the ground into dancing formations. Sal trees cast long shadows on the window, swaying with the wind. Meera looked out at the half-moon and the silvered clouds floating around it. Leaves continued to rustle; at times they crackled loudly and then became noiseless, as if caught by some invisible breeze.

Emre was no longer on guard. He had left behind other boys, after ensuring Meera's hands and mouth were strapped tight. Meera knew that the forest was full of rhesus monkeys, so the unquiet night shouldn't have bothered her. Nonetheless, she struggled to untangle her thoughts, focusing on the shifting sounds. The crackling of leaves grew louder, then stopped entirely, and she heard firm human footsteps on the wooden stairs leading to the corridor outside her room. Her heart began to race.

She looked around the room: the ashtray lying on the table in front of her, the deck of cards, the leftover food.

The footsteps were close now. Louder, louder—and then they passed, the sound fading to the other end of the corridor. Meera exhaled, relief flooding her veins. She wondered if it had been one of the boys, but she knew they didn't use the alley behind the building.

Then the footsteps returned.

They were creeping from the far end of the corridor back to Meera's room, fast, heavy, reckless. The doorknob twisted and a man crept inside the room, cutting short the shaft of moonlight leaking through the window. The figure walked ahead, gazing at the petrified face of the girl.

Haza…

Meera's feet turned cold at once. She looked into his gritty eyes and the loose bags hanging beneath them. He kneeled beside her, laying his hands upon her neck and sniffing close to her lips.

'Here you are,' he said, laughing to himself.

She tried to scream, but the gag muffled the sound. He pulled her body from the chair. Her cold skin smarted against his coarse beard, and he moved his head down to her cleavage and, with both hands, ripped her shirt.

'Shush,' he said, but her cries were swallowed by the cloth. He moved his hands across her body, thrusting his hardened organ against her abdomen, grinning as her scanty clothing impeded his progress. He moved down, biting the skin of her thighs.

She tried to scream again, and he laughed. He bit down hard, grinning as her body shook, tears welling-up in her eyes. He was enjoying the game.

Then, a high-pitched sound. Haza rose, lifted his cell phone, muttering under his breath, and rejected the call. Barely a moment later, his phone quivered again, and this time, with a final glance at Meera, he answered.

Meera screamed, the sound breaking past the gag, and Haza grabbed a handful of her hair. But she only screamed louder, the saliva bubbling around her gag.

Swearing, Haza hung up and slapped the girl in the face.

'You won't understand, will you?' he grunted.

Then, he squashed her breasts against her ribcage and, pulling all her clothes aside, slid his finger inside her, lubricating the dry cervix with saliva and stretching his lower back to spread her legs on the cold floor.

She beat her head on the floor as he thrust himself inside her and released a long sigh. His abrasive hands tore into her arms while he slid his organ in and out.

Someone slammed a fist against the door.

Haza sped up and tried to finish, but the person on door banged again.

'Haza, police!' the voice at the door exclaimed.

Haza cursed and stood up, leaving the girl shaking on the floor, and put on his pants. He spat on the floor and approached the door. Slowly, he unlocked, wiping the sweat from his forehead, and eased the door open an inch.

'What happened?' he asked the two men on the doorstep: Sumer and Hoque.

Sumer took a quick step forward and pushed with his shoulder and opened the door. Haza fell back, almost tripping, and Sumer and Hoque stormed into the room.

Haza righted himself and took a step back, eyeing Sumer. 'What are you waiting for? Hurry up, pack the guns,' he said.

'There is no police,' Sumer said, staring at Haza.

'Then what are you doing here? Go out! Can't you see I'm in the middle of something, fools!'

Sumer didn't move; he just stood there, his eyes fixed on Haza's face. Hoque, meanwhile, walked to Meera's side and pulled a blanket from the bed, throwing it over her. Then, he kneeled down, feeling her nose for a breath. Sumer joined him as Hoque carried her to the sofa.

'What are you doing?! Get out!' Haza shouted.

Emre and Sahil burst through the door.

'I told you this pig doesn't deserve us,' Emre said.

Sumer turned and, in three quick steps, crossed the distance between him and Haza. He seized the old man's collar and slammed him against the wall, his face trembling, eyes ablaze with hatred and disgust.

Haza peered back startled, trying to speak, but it was

too late—Sumer grabbed his head and slammed it against the concrete wall.

'What're you doing this for? A Hindu girl!' Haza screamed. Blood poured down the back of his head. 'Don't be fooled by principles. It's okay, you too can enjoy her afterwards. I didn't stop any of you. Make her your mistress.'

Sumer slammed his fist into the man's face.

'Scoundrels like you deserve no place in any religion. I made a mistake by trusting you last time. I should've killed you right there. You deserve no life, not for any country,' Sumer growled.

Haza slumped to the floor, blood leaking down his face. 'I made you,' he managed to whimper, 'you're nothing without me.'

Sumer stood over the old man and, slowly, placed a knee upon his heaving chest. He kneeled and wrapped both hands around Haza's throat.

'I trusted you, did everything for you, and here you are, making mistresses, staining the mission. You don't deserve another chance.' Sumer's hands tightened, the pool of blood growing beneath Haza's head.

Haza's eyes grew wide, red veins pushing towards his pupils. He struggled feebly, hands clawing at Sumer's arms; his body shook terribly. The old sack wobbled, beat his limbs on the floor, and gasped once more before falling silent forever.

Sumer staggered back and, after a moment, screamed. Tears were rolling down his cheeks. The three other boys stood silently, staring at Haza's motionless body. There were no questions and no answers—no words from anyone.

'Here is your chance to avenge his crimes against your

family,' Sumer said to Emre, his voice flat. 'Cut him into pieces and bury him with your hands. You've got four hours before sunrise.'

∞

The strange silence persisted. Meera finally rose and washed herself in the bathroom. She locked herself in there for almost two hours. Emre and Hoque had gone out to dig a hole for Haza, slightly distant from the highway among the sal trees, and Meera wondered whether they'd actually cut him into pieces or not. Only they, or the soul of Haza, knew. The boys said nothing about it to Sumer when they returned.

Meera looked at herself in the mirror. Her eyes were full of humiliation and her legs would not stop trembling. She bit her hand, trying to bury the emotional pain under her physical pain, and listened to the conversation of the men outside.

Emre, returning from calm, said to Sumer, 'He wasn't your real father.'

Sahil added, 'You did the right thing.'

Meera slumped to the floor, unable to figure out how she would go outside and face Sumer and Hoque, the two who had seen her naked on the floor. She pulled her hair aside and threw up. Outside, the men went quiet.

Sixteen

Mrs Sharma had escaped her house that morning by claiming she had an appointment at a nearby clinic. She had hired an autorickshaw to take her through the industrial district, down to the offices of Shah Industries. Angst and determination masked her beautiful face as she held her wallet tight, her face covered with a veil. She peered out at the traffic on the road and felt a commotion inside her chest.

How could the rest of the world just go on normally while hers had fallen apart?

'Here, eighty rupees,' she said, handing a hundred to the driver as he pulled up outside the building of Shah Textiles. The man leaned over his till, looking for change, but Mrs Sharma had already briskly walked away.

She wiped the sweat from her temple as she entered the lobby, uncovering her face. Her eyes scanned the place—the modern interior, the briefcases, the suits, the masses of English speakers. She took a corner of her veil and tangled it between her fingers. The lady behind the reception desk beckoned her forward, but Mrs Sharma bit the inside of her lip, translating a string of Hindi words into English in her head. She started with the first word—'I'—and then uttered the remainder in her own language. The receptionist smirked, her wry eyes clocking Mrs Sharma's decent clothes and jewellery and, alongside them, her messy hair and the dark circles under her eyes.

'So, you're a relative of Meera Sharma?' the receptionist enquired, forwarding her info to Namita's office. Mrs Sharma stared at the young woman.

'I'm her mother.'

The receptionist forced a smile, but Mrs Sharma noticed her trembling. 'I'll let Ms Shah know you're here.'

Inside her office, Namita Shah thought of dodging Meera's mother. She could have the receptionist tell Mrs Sharma that she was in a meeting, or out for lunch. But no; that would only be delaying the inevitable. With a heavy sigh, Namita confirmed the appointment. She took a sip of water. Escaping from the victim's family would only deepen the turmoil, but explaining her case and winning the mother over could help her—and thus her company's—image in the media.

She stood, pacing for a moment, trying to think of some pacifying opening line and cleared the stationery from her desk. She glanced in the mirror, fixing her hair so as to expose the dressing on the side of her head.

Mrs Sharma walked in without knocking, and the two women looked at each other indifferently. Namita rose, forced a smile, and greeted Mrs Sharma with a side hug. 'Please, sit down.'

Mrs Sharma did so, not saying anything.

'How're you feeling?' Namita enquired, glancing at Mrs Sharma's face. 'Would you like something? Water? Tea?'

Finally, Mrs Sharma looked up at the bandage on the side of Namita's head and the scratches on her face, hidden somewhat under a layer of expensive concealer. 'Thanks,' she said at last, 'I don't need anything. I'm here to talk.' She twisted her fingers.

Namita quivered and pulled up her shoulders. 'Yeah, sure.'

'Do you hate us?' Mrs Sharma asked.

Namita frowned. 'What?'

'Look, I'm a woman, and I understand you've gone through a lot. Your failed marriage, your kids gone…'

Namita stared at her, scarcely believing what she was hearing.

'Whatever relationship our husbands shared was just business; we did not mean to interfere in your matters. My husband's friendship with Mr Ajeet was as bogus as his friendships with his other clients. I know he hurt your ego—maybe you look down on him, or think he's a shallow agent—that's fair, I get it. But it has nothing to do with my family. Your kids are grown up too. How would you feel if your daughter disappeared and never came back?'

Namita just gaped. 'I'm sorry,' she said at last. 'I don't understand. What do you mean to say?'

Mrs Sharma sighed. 'Look, if you've done this to seek revenge on our family, you've won already; we're destroyed.' The lines upon her forehead deepened. 'Please give me my daughter back.'

'What? You're accusing *me* of all this?' Namita said, thumping her hands flat upon her desk.

Mrs Sharma began to wail, clasping her hands. Tears began to bubble from her eyes. 'She'll die. Please.'

Namita stared at her, mouth agape. She tried to say something but stopped herself. She swept her hair behind her ears and exhaled, looking around and rising from her chair. 'Mrs Sharma,' she said slowly, 'I respect your feelings, but you're crossing the line. I don't want to continue this conversation. You should leave.'

'It was your factory and your responsibility. How could you not know the village your own folks established? Who would possibly dare to attack you there? It doesn't even make sense.'

'The police are investigating,' Namita said coldly, turning and placing a hand on the side of her hip. 'Nothing can be said until their reports arrive. We're trying our best.'

'Trying? How? Sitting in your air-conditioned office, making money? My child is suffering out there,' Mrs Sharma yelled, rising to face her. 'I know women like you; you can't see someone happy because you're devastated yourself. You have two days. If you do not bring back my daughter, you'll face consequences.'

'Please don't force me to call security,' Namita said, unwavering.

Mrs Sharma rose, clutching her wallet, and marched towards the door. 'Call whomever you want to. I won't spare you till I get my child.'

Namita watched her go, exhaling as she left. The glass door swung in and out before becoming steady at last.

∞

Officer Yadav peered around the Saharanpur flea market. His eyes glinting, he walked behind the wooden handicrafts garage where Nandu usually loitered; the police knew that the gang member used it to smuggle items for Raju.

'You're not afraid to call us here?' the officer said.

Nandu turned, wincing; he'd been creeping towards the back door of the garage. He straightened, brushing himself off.

'What's there to be afraid of when we both know everything about each other?' Nandu said, eyeing the cops. 'But you should be worried about what you don't yet know.'

The officer lowered his eyebrows. 'What do you mean?'

A frenzied mass of cars, cart vendors, scooters and autorickshaws followed a slow-moving tractor down the market road. Nandu looked around and moved deeper into the garage, making sure that no one nearby saw him talking to the cops.

'I asked around for the girl everywhere, but this isn't the work of Raju's gang or their rivals. Besides, we supply 8 millimetre pistols, 7.65 millimetre bore improvised pistols and these are mostly used by local boys to commit petty crimes of ten to fifty thousand.'

Subordinate Rana stepped forward. 'You mean, the rifle description we gave you…'

'The AK-47—yes, we order them from Farrukhabad when a customer demands it but, since they're bought by only a few people, we know all our buyers by name. It's an expensive weapon, sahib. It wouldn't be used to rob a bus for a few thousand rupees.' Nandu raised an eyebrow as he fumbled for his lighter. He lit a cigarette and then peered back at the officer, frowning. 'The make and model of the gun you showed me in the sketches don't resemble the ones we smuggle from

Farrukhabad. I can tell those were assembled in a different market and cost more than ours.'

Officer Yadav stared back at Nandu, scrutinizing his features, trying to ascertain the authenticity of his words. 'You know the consequences if this turns out to be a lie?' he said evenly, rubbing the back of his head.

'Why would I lie? This new group is as much trouble for our business as it is for you,' Nandu said.

The officer glanced at his subordinate and inhaled. 'Okay, you can go,' he said, waving Nandu away.

And Nandu immediately slunk away across a row of milkweed bushes behind the garage.

The officer ran a hand through his narrowly trimmed beard and pressed his tongue against the inside of his lips. Then, after a pause, he said, 'As usual, there's a story behind the story. I want to look at Namita's statements again. Get me in touch with the headquarters of Haridwar city.'

'Sure, sir,' Subordinate Rana said. With that, he turned and headed back out into the sun-drenched market.

Seventeen

The sound of locking a door and approaching footsteps woke Meera from her sleep. She quivered, shuffling backward, and propped her back against the stiff couch where she'd passed out last night.

'She's up,' said Emre.

Meera looked at him and sighed. The striped bedsheet under her smelled of phenyl and vomit. She touched her rumpled hair, still disoriented, and pressed her hands over her heavy eyes. Memories from the night prior came rushing back in fragments, and her eyes shot open. Through the gaps between her fingers, she saw Sumer's olive-green jacket hanging on the wooden peg behind the closed door.

She pulled her hands down from her face, feeling both relieved and embarrassed by the thought of his presence.

'Feeling better?' enquired Sumer.

She shuddered and lowered her head, her hair falling across her face. At once, she felt her abdomen unclench, and the pain there faded. *Weird*, she thought, *how nerves cannot feel spiritual wounds.* She tilted her head towards Emre.

'I'm hungry,' she said.

The four men looked at her discreetly.

Emre passed on his cup of tea to her. 'I'll get you something. Have this for now,' he said.

Sumer spoke gently from across the room. 'Everything is taken care of.'

Really, everything *was* taken care of. She looked at the patch where Haza had died, finding no sign of blood, and then glanced over at the four men, each of them easy and relaxed. It was as if Haza had never existed. Meera rose and limped towards the washroom.

There, she closed the door and pressed her ear to the wooden surface of the door. Hoque and Sumer did not often talk, but now they murmured to one another about Haza's grave. Meera sighed and turned away, moving to the sink to splash water on her face and put her hair up in a bun. The door of the room outside opened and shut as Hoque and Sumer left together. She then strolled out of the washroom and settled back on the couch. Sahil was flipping channels on the television, his eyebrows arching as he paused on a retro action movie.

Emre lay water and food upon the table in front of Meera. She looked at the food and then at the teen. He smiled at her. Strange. They weren't treating her as a hostage any more; her hands weren't tied, and she didn't need permission to use the restroom now.

An hour later, Sahil switched off the television when footsteps echoed on the staircase. Sumer and Hoque entered the room, their attitudes harmonious. Meera looked at them and felt an uneasy prickle on her skin once again. She placed the blanket around her shoulders and eyed them suspiciously.

'We're leaving in an hour,' Sumer said to Meera, and then he looked at the others.

The men silently consented. Despite the chaos wreaking havoc within every individual there, they knew they had to leave this place before any flies started droning over Haza's grave.

'Pack your stuff and do not risk leaving anything behind. I'll meet you at the bus station,' Sumer said, reaching for his rifle and slipping it into the nearby duffel.

An hour later, Emre led Meera out of the room. Hoque followed them at a brief distance. Sumer and Sahil stayed behind in the room to check for any evidence that had been left, but when they found none, they left too.

Meera wore her veil, covering three-quarters of her face, and walked through a crowd, pretending to be a pilgrim. Emre whispered in her ear, explaining how he and Hoque had cleaned the smears of blood from the room's walls.

Meera glanced at him and smiled; his gentle narration soothed her.

∞

Inside the state-run bus to Dehradun, Meera and her captors sat in pairs; the partners had been decided by Sumer. Emre and Meera sat in the fourth row, while Hoque and Sahil sprawled in the block of three seats on the other side of the aisle and Sumer lay by himself in the rear seat at the end of the aisle. They didn't talk, or even look around throughout the journey. The other passengers—mostly pilgrims, day labourers and students—bustled in and out as the bus paused in hamlets and small towns along its way.

The sun had begun to sink slowly in the sky and only a few passengers were left on board. The wind grew colder as the bus passed the border of Uttarakhand and climbed towards Himachal, dashing through hills and curved cliffsides. Meera glanced at Emre's lethargic face; he was struggling to stay alert enough to guard her. She looked out of the window. A flock of birds flew past, heading deeper into a verdant valley, and then disappeared behind a hill. *Heading for home*, Meera thought sadly.

The vehicle pulled over next to a roadside restaurant. The driver rose from his seat, announcing a break of twenty minutes, and climbed out of the bus. Cold air rushed in as the passenger door opened, and people began to move out. Meera looked at the facade of the shabby restaurant beside the mountain road. It reminded her of her village: dry stone walls, slanting timber roofs and filler stones supported by chains at the base to match the surface of the road.

Hoque and Sahil got off to buy cigarettes. Sumer jumped out too, and followed them to purchase a newspaper from the counter.

Emre took Meera out after all the seats had been vacated. Through the narrow alley, he walked her securely towards the restrooms. She looked at Sumer from across the crowd as he leafed through a newspaper—his face expressionless, unlike the others in his group. Suddenly, he turned and caught Meera looking at him. She quickly turned her head away.

Hoque and Sahil smoked cigarettes on a wide veranda nearby. A yellow bulb glowed above them, and masses of moths and mosquitoes buzzed around it. They talked and laughed lowly. Emre bought water and snacks. The evening turned darker with each passing minute. On the road in front of the restaurant, several vehicles zoomed past, their headlights flickering like fire beetles, moving further through the blackened valley and getting lost in the mountain's curves.

The bus driver finished his last sip of masala tea and rose from the restaurant bench to get back to his duty. Passengers began to report back aboard. The sound of the diesel engine, squeaking and shifting, reverberated through the calm valley as the vehicle pulled out of the mud patio and headed into the evening.

Through the night, the breeze from the valleys flowed fresh, pouring the beauty of sleeping green lands on the deadened travellers. Emre nodded off in his seat. Sahil and Hoque were partly listless too. Meera peeped around and straightened her neck when she felt as if someone was watching. She looked around again—Sumer was glaring at her. *He's a goddamn reptile,* she thought, and immediately sat straight in her seat.

∞

Several snow-capped peaks emerged in the bluish-white and yellow distance, the rising sunlight swallowing the darkness. The snow-tipped tops flickered, as if upset at being woken from their sleep. At lower elevations, creepers and wildflowers maintained their territory as shields of pine trees ran on both sides of the road, homes to macaques and Himalayan langurs.

As planned, the five of them descended from the bus at gaps of a few miles from one another before the boundary of the town of Choupal. The first one to land, Sumer hiked up to reach Sahil and Hoque a few miles down, and together, they waited for the third unit, Emre and Meera, to arrive.

The population board at the front of the town read '7800'. Beneath this figure was written, 'Welcome to the home of cedar trees'. In terraces on the hills around the town, wheat and seasonal vegetables grew in bursts of vibrant colour.

Emre lifted the duffel bag and hiked downhill, his eyes heavy after a disturbed sleep last night; he had watched the girl several times in between his catnaps. He pressed down his tousled hair and shrugged his aching shoulders. Meera's spine was rigid too, but her head felt lighter than it had been last night. She looked up into the clear sky and then closed her eyes, throwing her head back. Village women were collecting dried wood from the forest up ahead, and the smell of burning wood from the houses nearby was rich in the air.

Looking at the bird perching on a high pine, Meera said, 'Is it a bee-eater or a purple sunbird?'

'It's green, it can't be a purple sunbird, no?' Emre laughed.

'Yes, it's a bee-eater. See the emerald green fuzz and the black hoop around his neck?'

Emre peered at the bird as it fluttered and flew away. 'Yes, it is. I've seen it once in the Suleiman Hills,' he said.

'The Suleiman Hills? Where are they?' she asked.

'They're, err, in south India. A small range of hills,' he said quickly, and then walked ahead.

Strange, Meera thought, noting the shift in his tone. A cool gust from the west stroked her skin. She held her veil tighter and followed Emre, trekking slowly even as the boy hurried down.

Near the bottom, they found Sahil and Hoque resting on

the side of the road with their luggage. Hoque was smoking a cigarette while Sahil glanced at Emre before continuing to hum and carve figures into the dirt with a branch. *They don't seem tired*, Meera thought to herself, trying to stop panting. *Of course, they're used to such rough conditions.*

Above her, a family of macaques stared at them from a cedar branch, the mother grasping her infant, anxious about the human arrivals.

Sahil paused his carving and told Meera, 'You can sit.'

'I don't think it's a safe place; they are too many of them,' she said.

Hoque chuckled. 'You're scared of monkeys? We've got sticks, stones *and* guns in here.'

'No, I'm not letting you hurt them,' she said sourly.

'Wait until they steal your stuff. They pinched my clothes once and his underwear too.' Emre chuckled, pointing at Sahil, who pounced upon him. The two boys fell in the dirt, rolling and laughing.

Sumer lay nearby, resting his head on his bag; his body was on the roadside gravel. He looked at Meera who stood nearby, and then closed his eyes, his face perpendicular to the sky. In the near distance, a flock of birds took to the skies, disappearing into the clouds. The monkey family chewed on berries and wild seeds, the sounds of their munching breaking the silence.

Looking at Meera from his place, Sumer spoke, 'You're okay?'

She nodded, rather shaken by the sudden question.

Sumer rose from the ground and cleared his throat. 'You can go home,' he said.

Meera looked at him in disbelief. '*Home?* My home?' she stuttered.

'Yes, *your* home,' Sumer said slowly. 'You can go. I've called one of my men; he'll take you to Delhi,' he said.

She stared at him.

'We never wanted that daft to bring you here in the first place. We're not kidnappers,' Emre said, jumping up from the ground. Sumer eyed him. Emre fell silent.

The wind around Meera held itself momentarily, and so did everything else—the voices, faces and her senses. It was as if she had been pulled against gravity in the middle of a free fall. She inhaled, and then held her breath.

'Look, girl, we've got nothing against you,' Hoque continued in his typically heavy tone. 'You were in the wrong place at the wrong time. But you're a wise girl; we expect you to remain silent about everything. None of this has to get out. Nothing happened to you, you never saw us, and you'll be safe, I promise.' He looked into her eyes.

A man walking from the town stopped near them. Meera stared at him as he shook hands with Sumer and then with Hoque. His eyes were red at the corners and showed yellow teeth as he smiled. His shabby clothes stank, and Meera stepped away. He scratched his messy hair and then rubbed his neck, glancing at Meera.

'He'll take you home,' Sumer said.

'I'm not going with him,' she shot back.

Hoque glared at her.

'I'll go by myself!'

Sumer took a step forward. 'No, you can't go alone.'

'I was right; you're bothering too much about her. She'll

inform the police as soon as we release her,' Hoque said, tightening his fist. 'Girl, that pighead is dead, your revenge is met. We're being nice to you. Do not make us regret this decision. Our eyes will be on you, so anything you say, or hint at—well, you'll face the consequences.'

'You're lying. You're not releasing me but sending me off with this man for God knows what this time. I'm not a fool. I won't fall for your cheap tricks!' Meera shouted. The new man glanced at Sumer.

'I guess I was wrong about you,' Sumer said. Sighing, he stepped forward, grabbed Meera by the arm, and dragged her into the trees.

She cried out, but no help came. The four men followed close behind.

Eighteen

A great truth—one as tall and vast as a mountain—may weigh nothing, but even the smallest of lies can obsess a person. The aphorism wrapped itself around Meera's head as she stared at the four boys in the middle of the forest, her eyes open and her lips pressed tight. The air was cold beneath the dense screen of pines, the darkness gentle. Dried autumn leaves crackled underfoot as she took a step back, glancing at Emre.

'So, what were you saying?' Sumer snapped, his fingers still digging into her elbow.

Meera jerked her arm out from his grip and looked intently at Sahil and Emre. 'I thought you were different from Haza, but you're all the same,' she yelled.

Hoque grunted. 'Aye…we saved you!'

'Saved me? How? You brought me here, tied me and waited for Haza to come and rape me! It was all your fault. You made it happen. If you knew he was a pig, you should've killed him a long time ago,' she said. 'How many girls did you let him enjoy so far? Huh?'

'I understand the level of dishonour he brought to you,' Sumer said softly.

'Will that allow me to forget what happened? Every second of it will live with me till I die. And you're right: I won't hide. I'll tell the police what happened here and make sure you answer for your sins. I won't hide.' She glared at Hoque.

'How dare you?' Hoque uttered hoarsely.

'And you! Suleiman Hills are not in the south. I'm pretty sure they're in Pakistan,' she said, looking at Emre.

Sumer gestured for the new man to move forward. 'Take her.'

'Get off!' Meera shrieked.

'He'll take you home safely,' Sumer said.

'Why should I trust you?'

'Because you've got no choice,' Hoque said, shaking his head.

'I'll leave alone, or you can shoot me and get away with everything.'

The man dragging Meera froze, and stillness consumed the scene.

Hoque stepped forward. 'As you wish,' he said, and he pulled a pistol out from his waist and pressed the barrel against her forehead.

'This is all you can do, cowards!' she shouted. The rage from her deeper-self sparkled; her once-submissive eyes were now burning with hatred.

'I should've done this much earlier,' Hoque hissed, scowling at her.

Sweat broke upon her skin. 'I pray to God that your mothers and sisters never know this side of you,' she said.

Sumer shoved Hoque quickly as he pulled the trigger. The bullet zipped through the air, and a cacophony of cries rang out as a hundred birds burst out from the treetops into the sky. Meera recoiled, shock warping her frame and her eyes flaring with doubt as she checked herself twice, ensuring she was alive.

Sumer clutched Meera's arm and pulled her away. 'I changed my mind. Forget about going home. You'll see how cowards live. I thought I'd help you, but you turned out to be too ungrateful.'

She looked at him, shaking.

'You're making a mistake,' Hoque called after him.

'I'm fixing my mistake,' Sumer snapped back. He turned to the new man; who was standing alone, evidently confused. 'You can go. I'll deal with her.'

Emre and Sahil lifted their bags and followed Sumer deeper into the woods. Muttering to himself, Hoque pushed Meera forward; his pistol was still in his hand.

∞

Following a narrow stream through the valley, the group arrived at a house—or rather, a bungalow—surrounded by spruce. The front lawn jutted out towards a pond that ran parallel to it, and a tennis court peeped out of the backyard. White walls and carved wooden doors opened out on to another lawn in front of the bungalow, which was fenced by bushes and seemed more private. A man walked out of the front door in a police uniform, a big goofy smile on his face and a turban wrapped around his head. Meera thought he looked like Raunak Singh, a security guard at her office. How strange—all of her past seemed like a different world now. He crossed the narrow bridge across the pond and greeted Sumer warmly.

Meera eyed his turban and the service stars upon his shoulders as he greeted the other men in the group. Then, he looked at her. Clinging on to Sumer's instructions, she did what the others had done, greeted him with a salaam, pretending to be one of them.

'Where is the jeep?' Sumer asked.

'In the backyard. Follow this trail and you'll see my man waiting there,' the man in the uniform said, pointing at a muddy trail around the pond. 'She's with you?' He glanced sceptically at Meera. 'I was told about five men.'

Emre chuckled nervously. 'You think she's less than a man?'

'I see.' The uniformed man laughed and waved as the group moved away.

∞

The jeep moved north on the highway, passing through countless Himachal townships and villages. Hoque did not want to see the girl, and thus, took the front seat next to the driver. The rest four riders sat in the back seats, facing one another. All of them were silent, except for the growling wind that thumped at the canopy of the gypsy vehicle. Again, Meera tried to connect the dots between the boys, the uniformed officer, and the appalling rapist—if not money, what could have brought these men together?

The driver of the jeep, a middle-aged man with a decent beard, also in a police uniform, hadn't said a word. His eyes were sharp, seeming to observe everything around him, but his demeanour was relaxed. He crossed the checkpoints without inquiry, thus clearing a passage for his armed passengers.

At a fuel station near the town of Narkanda, Meera walked up to Emre as he rinsed his hands under a tap. He was lathering his face gently with soap. After that he ran his fingers through his hair and squinted at his soft acne in a dirty mirror.

'So, we're never going to talk?' she said nimbly.

He glanced at her but said nothing, then walked back towards the jeep.

Meera ran after him. 'I'm sorry I spoke about those mountains,' she said. 'I was scared about who you might be.'

He spoke bitterly. 'And you aren't scared now of what we might be?'

She gaped at him and, despite everything, began to laugh. 'I don't know,' she managed, still laughing. 'I really don't.'

Emre looked at her, apparently unwilling to say or ask her anything else.

'I'm only wondering if we will make a stop somewhere tonight,' she said at last.

'Yeah, we will,' he said, turning away, 'in twenty minutes.'

Nineteen

The terrace where Sunny spent many evenings with Meera, discussing the ruts of home and life, now seemed empty. He sat there alone gazing at the city lights and the dark purple sky. Trains ran on elevated tracks in the distance and he counted the north-bound trains against the south-bound. Finally, failing to recall his tally, he rubbed his forehead. He'd had had too much to drink. He laid on the swinging bench, closing his eyes. His senses swayed back and forth along with his body on the swing. He remembered his mother telling him that morning that Meera was alive, and that she had spoken to her in her dreams. Blurred images ran through his mind, and he felt himself choke, intoxication forcing him into an alternate reality. A shadow, like that of his sister's, walked from the edge of the terrace, moving towards him. He wobbled and threw up. The moon appeared from behind silver clouds.

Disoriented, Sunny rose and headed downstairs to his room. The sound of his stumbling footsteps through the living room broke the eerie silence of the house. His car keys clattered on the key hook behind the door as he prepared to leave. His vision was swimming and the skin around his neck was damp and sticky; he staggered on, grasping for his cell phone, but he was unable to find it. He shrugged and decided he could make it back without it, and he dragged himself into the elevator. He got off at the basement parking lot, and strolled towards his car.

The traffic was heavy, and Sunny drove unsteadily—switched lanes, sped up, forced breaks—towards a house in the upper side of Saket, where, he was sure, lived the answers to all his questions.

The lights in the bungalow were dim, reflecting the beauty of its form against the backdrop of the evening. A security guard in the cabin to the side of the front door waved Sunny down as he stumbled forward and held up his hand.

'Call your madam.' The pilot said.

'Who are you?' the guard, a uniformed man in his mid-forties, asked.

Sunny looked at the man as though his patience was wearing thin. The odour of alcohol was rising from his body as he tried to explain, but the words came out garbled and incomprehensible. He tried again—then, seeing the guard roll his eyes, he punched him in the face and sprang forward, running towards the iron gate. Two other men ran out from the courtyard to block him. Sunny tried to duck, but he fell, and the men were upon him almost immediately, pulling his arms behind his back and dunking his face into the garden soil.

'She knows me, faggots! Let me go!' the pilot yelled, jostling against the grip of the man behind him.

Namita strode out of the house. 'What on earth is happening here?' she snapped, glaring at the first security guard. When the guard stuttered, she peered down at the man writhing on the ground.

Her face softened. 'What're you doing here, Sunny?'

'I want to talk to you! Just for a minute,' Sunny uttered, gasping for breath and spitting mud.

'Leave him,' Namita said.

'Madam, he's drunk as hell,' one man said.

She walked ahead. 'I'll handle it,' she said.

A maid from inside the bungalow ran to help him, but Namita lifted him alone, his arm draped around her shoulders. The maid walked anxiously alongside them, holding doors open as Namita dragged Sunny into the house and pulled the curtains of the living room. Namita lay him upon a couch.

The sleek lights hanging from the ceiling illuminated the tarnished wood and chiffon curtains hanging on three sides of the room. In a corner, vintage candlesticks rested beside a row of crystal beaded vases. The gentle fragrance of coconut and vanilla spun in the air, obscuring even the stench of alcohol rising from the boy. Namita looked down cluelessly at him. She peered over her reading glasses and pulled her nightgown tight around her before gesturing for the maid to bring some water.

A stack of papers from the office lay jumbled on the table in front of the couch where Sunny lay. Namita cleared them noiselessly as the maid returned with a glass of water on a tray. The two women sat Sunny up, and the maid held the glass to his lips.

'You know where Meera is?' Sunny asked, the words slurring.

Namita moved away. 'Why do you think I'm the reason

behind all your problems?' she said.

Sunny yelled, trying to stand up, 'Look at me and tell me you don't know.'

'I don't know.'

'Madam, you want me to call someone?' The maid grabbed the landline, visibly panicked.

'Aniket. Call Aniket,' Namita said nervously.

'Yeah, call him! What would he do? Fuck you? You're happy that my sister is gone, aren't you? You can grope at her man now,' the pilot said, first rash and then, at once, bursting into laughter. 'You fucked up our lives.'

Namita pushed him away, her eyes welling. 'What can I say? I'm a successful woman. Since I've aspired to more than this world allows, I have to survive the judgements of this society for the rest of my life,' she said, rubbing her sudden tears away. 'You know, all this time I've been wondering why those thieves took your sister and not me. I almost wish I'd been taken. After all, I had to return and suffer while she's the tragic hero, the noble sacrifice.' Namita blew her nose and looked at Sunny. 'I admit, I was responsible for the safety of my staff, and I failed her there. But you don't know how it felt to be held at gunpoint and see my people beaten up and dragged away.'

The boy stepped back, letting the woman sob. Then, she moved forward and took his hand, a tear curling down her cheek. 'I wish I could go back and change things, but it's too late. People who sacrifice themselves—like your sister—are different. They don't just die like other people. She will remain in our hearts and we do owe our lives to her.'

'I want to believe you, just tell me how.' Sunny shouted

and looked at her face. 'How should I?'

At once, everything began to feel blurred and delusional to him. He grabbed his head.

'I understand what it means to lose your family. I've lost mine too. I promise you I won't give up on her. We'll do everything to bring her back.'

For a minute, there was silence—a sense of awkwardness and belonging, which slowly faded. The two provoked individuals melted into one another, arms grasping one another, tears falling freely. The maid put down the landline receiver and left the room.

Twenty

At a cottage in Shoja, where the jeep's driver had pulled over for the night, Meera remained isolated from the group. The temperature in the valley continued to drop throughout the evening, as it did within the group. The boys went out with the driver to smoke and make a bonfire in the woods, while Meera walked around the empty cottage—*More of a dilapidated house than a cottage*, she thought—swathed in pine and deodar trees. The single electric bulb in the corridor flickered relentlessly, and the building had no heating or hot water. The concierges—an elderly couple from a village nearby—had given the jeep driver a heating rod for water when he'd arrived. Meera hung it in a bucket and began to prepare some water for a bath.

Inside the room, she lay back, thinking about her home and mulling over Sumer's proposal for her release. Perhaps, she thought, she had dug her own grave by judging the shabby man by his appearance. She rested her head upon her luggage, tears rolling down her cheeks.

Later that night, someone from the group eased into her room. He watched her for a moment, then turned to leave.

The burn scar on his neck gleamed under the flickering bulb before it ran out of power again.

∞

Clouds hovered over the well-lit canopy of the Seraj Valley. Birds flew in circular paths around hills and then merged into the trees. Emre walked to Meera's room and knocked on the door. She opened the door, peeking out.

'You need anything from the market? I'm going for groceries,' he said.

She looked around and spoke lowly, 'I do, but I'll pick it up myself.'

'They probably won't allow it, but let me check,' he said, turning away.

A while later, he returned and knocked on her door again. 'Sumer bhai will take you to the village. Be ready in fifteen minutes.'

'Okay,' she said, realizing that the men didn't trust Emre with her any more on account of him spilling important information.

Sumer arrived and wordlessly led Meera out. They walked along a mud lane, which was engraved with jeep tyre marks. Thick foliage covered the ground, and dry pine cones and spruce swept beneath their feet as they walked.

'Thank you for saving me,' Meera said after a while.

He didn't reply.

She wished to say more but, finding him unresponsive, she stayed silent. The sound of cicadas and birds persisted unbroken. *He's strange, resentful perhaps. Or maybe simply mournful. There's definitely something weird about him*, she told herself as they neared the village.

Meera visited a department store while Sumer remained outside, watching her.

'That's all?' he enquired when she strolled out of the store with a small bag.

'Yes.'

'We can buy something else if you need it,' he said.

'I'm fine,' she said, glancing at him.

He turned and began to walk back in the direction of the cottage.

'Are we staying here tonight?' she asked, hurrying to catch up.

'No.'

'That driver, he'll take us out of here?'

'Why are you asking?' he turned and stared at her. 'You need to know everything?'

She looked at him nervously. 'I was asking so I can be prepared.'

The lines upon his forehead deepened before he turned and began to walk again.

∞

Shoja to Kyelang: a seven and a half hour journey via the Leh-Manali highway. They passed dozens of quaint villages, lofty mountains and lakes as they went. Finally, the jeep crossed the threshold of Kyelang town late in the evening and, five miles on, they reached Spiti district.

The long journey had consumed them all. Now, at ten

thousand feet, they found themselves short of breath, starved of oxygen. Sheets of snow stretched from the low valleys to the top of the barren hills. The jeep driver turned around his vehicle and said goodbye to the boys before heading back in the direction of Choupal. Apparently, his job of carrying them through the barricades had ended.

Lights glowed in the distance. Meera followed the group as they wound their way on.

'Haza would've had a different plan,' Hoque said, wheezing.

Sumer scowled. 'Well, he's dead now,' he snapped, 'and maggots must've holed up inside his flesh by now, so we cannot ask him.'

Hoque paused, gasping for breath and staring at Sumer. 'You think it's funny? Have you thought of what will happen when Sukhbir confirms the gender of our new fifth person? We can't hide Haza's death for long.'

'So what?' Sumer grunted. 'No one will know anything unless we tell them. Our path has been guided. We do what is right, to him and to her. If you fear justice, brother, you can leave.'

'You're making a mistake,' Hoque said.

Emre jumped between the two. 'Okay, one thing at a time!' he said.

'I'm frozen already. We can discuss it in the room,' Sahil said, folding his arms.

Sumer glared at his men. 'Then do as I say.'

∞

A tough alliance, Meera thought, but they at least had an organized set of protocols, and each one abided by it, willing or not. The new room was made of light wood but was warm enough. She lay in a fine bed, looking at her fake ID. Fake photos, tourist faces, and momentary smiles—somehow, it had become normal for her. She even found herself relating to the girl on her bogus licence. She dressed like her when she knew they'd be taking her out in public and she equipped herself with answers Sumer had taught her to the questions someone might ask. Now, in her clean room, she prepared to sleep, her body still adjusting to the new altitude.

Just before dawn the next morning, a soft knock echoed on her door. Meera woke, shuddered, and carefully unchained the door.

Sumer glanced at her. He looked fresh and, for once, well rested.

'I was wondering if you wanted to go out,' he said. She looked at his sweatshirt and running shoes.

'Yes, I'll come,' she said slowly before closing the door again. Quickly, she washed her face and pulled on some clothes.

She hastened, her sluggishness gone at once, wondering whether she was in danger. She put on her jacket and lifted her small polybag of luggage, recalling Hoque's cold argument with Sumer last night.

She emerged from her room. 'Okay, let's go,' she said, and rushed out from the log cabin. Sumer followed, mystified.

A freezing gust of wind swept at her as soon as she stepped outside. She inhaled, the fresh fragrance of the Himalayas filling her lungs. She shivered due to the cold and at the sight:

the sun breaking through snow-capped peaks and illuminating every particle in its way. She blinked, watching mist-generated clouds skim across the ground. Light snow dust covered the grass, contrasting with the rich greens, and Meera turned to see Sumer watching her from the edge of the cabin portico; he walked with a relaxed gait. She turned away, the snow crunching under her feet.

'So, you are a routine runner,' Sumer said from behind her.

'Hoque is mad at me again?' she said, ignoring his statement.

'No.'

'Why are we here then?'

'I thought you needed to walk around. You've been grounded for days.'

'That's it?' She paused.

'Yes, that's it. Wait. Why did you bring your bag?' he said, snatching her polybag from her.

'I thought you were going to help me escape.'

He laughed; the sound was harsh to her ears.

She slowed down, panting, and he too slowed to a jog, following the bank of the Bhag River. She followed at a distance, halting at times, and was soon wheezing. He took the zigzag trail towards the Kardang Monastery and its religious flags, imprinted with a few signs.

Reaching the top of a hill, Meera sat on a low drystone wall, gaping at the white walls of the Buddhist monastery. 'Nine hundred years…can you believe how old this building is!' she exclaimed.

'Quite a historian,' Sumer said mockingly.

She ignored him and walked towards the building. He

watched as she explored the near and far-flung corners. She could have run, but for some reason, she didn't leave his sight.

The wind was stronger on the top of the hill, but Meera stood facing its direction; it felt amazing on her warmed-up body. Sumer began a set of exercises. The mist around them began to fade, banished by the rising sun on the horizon. She stared at the peaks cradling the distant sun, its light outlining the crest. A serene smile stretched upon her lips. She'd seen the sun rising in Delhi, but never had it looked anything like the sun rising in her village. This, though…

Her skin glowed like hot metal. Then, lying back on the drystone wall, she shifted her view to the prayer flags hanging upon the wires surrounding the monastery.

Sumer had moved on from light breathing and joint exercises to heavy cardio and stretches. By the time he had finished, the sun was bright and full in the sky. He wiped his forehead and came to sit by Meera's side.

'How long have you been doing these intense workouts?' she said.

'Since I was fourteen, I think.' He smiled.

'And the guns? How long have you been around them?'

'Twelve,' he said evenly. 'I began using them at sixteen, however.'

'Did you ever go to school?'

'I studied, but only the subjects I should. We all studied; each of us is competent in his field.'

'Competent? As in what…?'

He blinked several times and said, 'You can say I excel in chemistry.'

'Were you even born in India?'

She looked at him, seeing the expression on his face change. His eyes flared for a moment and then were blank. He turned away.

'Sorry, it's just that you don't look like you were born in this country—none of you do,' she said.

He rose and, without a word, began walking back towards the cabin.

∞

Inside her room, Meera thought about Sumer's reaction. She'd doubted their nationality since she'd first met them—their light brown eyes, pale skin tone and their accents contradicted the regular north Indian Hindi accent. She remained locked in her room until the afternoon. It was strange that no one checked on her or brought her food. She checked the door and found it unlocked. Peeping out and finding the hallway empty, she crept down the corridor and paused outside the next room. Silence, except for some muffled voices from the television. Starving and curious, she leaned down and put her eye to the keyhole. A man stood on the other side, blocking her sight. She pressed her ear to the door and heard a conversation in a language she didn't understand. The new man said something hushed and soft. Then, Sumer replied in the same foreign tongue, and she felt her head swim.

Not only had she dived into cold water, but she was swimming among sharks.

Someone approached the door from inside the room. She spun around, but she could make it only halfway back to her room when Emre appeared. He stopped, and they looked at each other, their faces pale. Through the narrow opening of the door, Meera caught a glimpse of the new man. He wore a black overcoat and was tall—about six and a half feet—and heavy-set. He had a long grey beard.

'I'm hungry, I was looking for you,' she said as he slid the door behind him shut.

'Go away. I'll come to you,' he grunted.

She nodded, her heart hammering in her chest, and returned to her room.

Twenty-one

Namita ignored the gaping faces of passers-by as her new Mercedes slid out of the mediocre colony gates. Some residents gawked from the neighbourhood lawns and some from their apartment's balconies. She stepped out in a high-neck fleece jacket, Louis Vuitton accessories and sunshades, her bandage still patching the left side of her head. Her secretary pushed the elevator button, and together, the two ladies headed towards the flat belonging to the Sharmas.

Inside the living room, she sat with two men, Mr Sharma and Aniket. Her eyes scanned the house, inspecting minor details like cushions and the cutlery set upon the dining table. Sunny walked out from his room and the woman's keen eyes paused at once. She blinked and looked down. Then, she glanced up, smiling at him. She believed the boy was done with her—for him, it had doubtlessly been just another hook-up.

Mrs Sharma stood behind the door of her bedroom, listening keenly.

The lady wearing the steep perfume began the conversation, her throat damp and eyes full of tears. Her secretary handed her a tissue and she wiped her eyes. Needless to say, she was skilled at waving white flags and weeping when necessary.

'Your loss is beyond words. I cannot tell you how guilty I feel, so please, let me help you a little with this,' she said. Her secretary pulled out a file and spread a cheque of fifty lakh rupees on the table.

Mr Sharma looked at Namita and adjusted his spectacles.

Aniket spoke from across the table. 'I appreciate your concern, but we don't need this, Namita. It was an accident, and you don't have to feel guilty.'

'Please accept it. You're going through a lot, and so is my company,' she said. 'At this moment, only we can help each other bring things back to normal. I've organized a press conference at my office the day after tomorrow. It'd be great if you would join us. Maybe it'll push the cops to invest more resources into the investigation when the media covers all of us.'

Mr Sharma said nothing, but nodded gently. As someone who'd seen enough of the world and dealt with its realities, a part of his heart had already accepted the death of his daughter. He'd been ignoring calls from his brothers and relatives who wanted funeral ceremonies to be conducted soon. Even if cremation wasn't possible, he needed to conduct a thirteen-day mourning period and shraddha ceremony at the end. Silently, he imagined the moment when he'd speak about it to his family, his wife especially.

'I don't know if the media will boost the pace of the investigation. What if it alarms the kidnappers and, out of panic, they end up doing something worse to Meera?' Aniket said, glancing at Sunny.

Mr Sharma turned his attention to the people sitting in his living room and tucked another thought of the funeral away. Even now, they were positive that she was alive.

Namita followed Sunny's gaze, expecting the pilot to join her side.

'Aniket is right,' Sunny said slowly, avoiding looking at Namita. 'We should postpone any contact with the press until the investigation bears some fruit. We know nothing about those people and how they're going to react if things are stirred the wrong way at this point.'

Mrs Sharma burst out from the bedroom in sobs.

Mr Sharma looked at his wife, quivered, and cleared his throat. Namita rose, while the lady of the house looked at her, eyes hard, tears still streaming down her cheeks.

Quietly, Sunny lifted the cheque lying on the table and gave it back to Namita. Then he rose and led the guests out to the elevator. Namita stared at him as the elevator door slid shut. She wanted to speak, but realized that her only chance to talk to him was gone. The pilot's mouth slackened and blankly, he watched her leave.

∞

Sumer knocked on Meera's door. It was late, but eventually, she eased the door open, holding the wooden flap firm as she peeked out at him. Of course, Emre had been reporting any news about her to Sumer, no matter how subtle or small, and he doubtlessly knew about her infiltration of their room that afternoon.

'I'll take you for a walk tomorrow morning,' Sumer said calmly.

'Why?' she asked, startled.

He smiled. 'Because I want a companion.'

'Why me? I don't even work out.'

'I don't like questions, least of all from you. See you at 5 a.m.'

He turned around to leave as she mumbled something under her breath.

He paused. 'Did I scare you this morning?'

'No.'

'So, you've got no reason to be afraid. I'll let you know when you should be.'

She looked at him, her eyes trying to read every line upon his face, while he shot her a smile and left.

∞

Snow reigned across the hills of Kyelang, the valley glistening in the morning light. The wind was somewhat calm, unlike the previous day, and dew shone on the grass. Soft orange hues burned like embers in the eastern sky. Sumer jogged along the riverbank, the sound of water flowing through ruffled rocks and small rapids piercing the quiet morning. Meera followed, lagging behind, but controlling her breath and maintaining the pace. The cold air circled inside her brain, and she felt her taut joints slackening and muscles stretching.

Arriving at the top of the hill, Sumer stood at the periphery of the monastery, quiet as ever, gazing at the light breaking through the peaks. Meera walked to the edge and stood away from him.

'You won't work out today?' she asked gently.

'I will, but first, we need to talk,' he said.

She raised an eyebrow.

'But before I speak, I need to make sure that you trust me.'

'I do,' she said, her expressions wavering.

He stepped forward and plucked out a fruit knife from the inner pocket of the girl's jacket.

'Why did you bring this then?' he snapped.

Her face turned pale and at once she recoiled.

'I know why you came to my room yesterday and, in fact, I wanted you to come,' he said, looking away. 'I would've sent you home that day. If only you had shown a bit of trust and realized what I had lost by losing my only family. Well, if you've got the nerve to call me a coward and offer me money, you should hear my price.'

She gripped the railing behind her firmly and retreated a step. 'How much?' she mumbled.

'How much is the price of faith? And fear?' he said, looking into her eyes.

She stepped back. 'What do you mean?'

'Take a guess and see if you can figure out who I am.'

She clutched the railing tightly, leaning away as he stepped forward.

'You're not a thief. You don't belong to this land, and Hindi isn't your native language.'

'And?'

'And you've got assault rifles, your skin is burnt. It's a chemical burn and you studied chemistry—radioactive chemistry, is it?'

'You're almost there.'

'You're an enemy,' she said softly, looking at him.

'If that simplifies everything. I'm a terrorist. That's what your country calls us.' He was close now, eyes fixed on hers.

Meera held her breath.

'I need to go.' She fumbled and turned around, preparing to run back to the room.

He didn't follow her. He just stood, watching blankly from the top of the hill as she disappeared round the bend.

∞

Inside her room, Meera thought about her reaction at the monastery over and over. Was it a fight or a flight response? It wasn't danger that she felt next to Sumer, she realized, but something else. Everything was messed up. She tried to open the door to her room and found it locked from the outside now. She could have easily wandered away on her own from the monastery, but she hadn't. She lay down in her bed, turned on the television, and tried to reckon what on earth made her come back to this room.

That afternoon, Emre struck at her door and pushed it open. Meera jumped up.

'I brought food,' he said, remaining in the doorway.

She took the bag of food and shut the door immediately.

Emre stared for a moment at the closed door, and finally shrugged. As long as she remained inside her room, she wasn't his problem. He whistled an anonymous song and walked away.

That evening, Sumer arrived again. He pushed past her

when she opened the door, her eyes wide and frame defensive. He glanced around the room before he sank into the futon near the bed.

Meera stared at him, while he calmly read her face.

'How does the morning walk feel?' he said.

She stood, clicking her nails swiftly against one another and gritting her teeth, as if facing a spectre.

'I asked you something.'

'You haven't finished what you started,' she said, cutting him off.

He looked away and scoffed. 'Are you desperate for my story or your release?'

'Both.'

He was silent for a moment. Finally, he looked up. 'You want to go out now?'

She nodded.

∞

The snowfall that afternoon had left an inch of white upon the ground. Lights from the local market caught upon the ice, glittering and casting multicoloured hues upon the snow. Meera walked beside Sumer through the flea market. There was no wind. Light flurries of snow swam through the air before settling on stalls or fabric covers. They walked to the end of the arcade and, finding the trail leading to the monastery completely covered with snow, turned back towards the street. Sumer lit a cigarette while Meera folded her arms, shivering.

Her teeth clattered as she spoke. 'Will you hurry up and say something before I freeze here?'

'I have a cigarette if you want,' he said, holding out his pack to her.

'Thanks, but I don't smoke.'

'I thought city girls did all kinds of stuff.' He smirked and took a puff.

'You're poorly informed, I'm afraid,' she said, looking at the pack. Then, she slipped out one roll and pressed it between her lips.

He eyed her. 'You've never smoked before, right?'

'I've never been raped either.'

He said nothing, but he watched as she took the lighter from his hand and tried to light her cigarette, nearly burning her brows.

An elderly man walking past them turned and looked at her. She stared back, blowing smoke at him, and the man left. She took another puff and began to cough.

'Easy!' Sumer laughed.

'What a cheap brand!' She gasped.

'This cheap brand keeps me going.' He smiled and held her cigarette as she continued to cough. 'To start, don't take the smoke that far down your throat. Feel the heat and aroma in your mouth, and then blow it out.'

She held the cigarette and followed his instructions but, unable to stop coughing, tossed it upon the ground.

'I don't need it,' she said, crushing its light under the tip of her shoe. He gawked at her and at the destroyed cigarette. Then, standing quietly and finishing his own, he led her towards a restaurant.

Inside the diner, he ordered some tea and scones for two. She followed him, her face covered, towards an isolated bench facing the far wall and sat down opposite him. Then she folded her arms upon the table and looked briefly out of the window, and then gazed at his face.

'Why are you looking at me like that? I won't kill you for wasting a cigarette,' he said.

'No, I'm just wondering how terrorists look like normal people. I'm walking down streets and having tea with one of them. No one would believe it.'

He smiled.

She looked out at the snow heaped on the ledge of the window. 'How come you fell into such a silly business?'

He looked away and took a deep breath. 'This silly business is called a holy war in my language and we, the soldiers.'

'What makes you think that killing innocents is holy?' She kept her eyes fixed on the table.

'War and sacrifice go hand in hand; there's nothing I can do to stop it. Yes, I don't intend to fight unarmed people, not unless I'm bound by orders. That's one thing I hate,' he said, the intensity in his eyes swelling.

'But you've killed people before, haven't you?'

He sighed. 'You know the answer.'

The server arrived and they fell silent. As soon as he left, they looked at each other grimly.

'How is it? Killing someone you don't even know?' she asked.

'It's not easy. When a bullet leaves the barrel, it kills two people: the target and the shooter. One's body, the other's conscience.'

'Why did you do it then? Why choose this life?'

'I didn't choose it. I was raised into it. Haza had been my handler for many years. If he hadn't picked me up from the streets of Herat, my fate would've been decided by hunger,' he said, twitching and looking around.

'Herat? As in Afghanistan?'

He nodded.

'Herat used to be an Islamic state before the intervention of the Soviets,' he said, holding his cup of tea and looking distant, his eyes shrouded in vagueness again. 'My mother was executed for breaking Sharia law. I don't remember her face precisely now, but she was beautiful—serene eyes and a pure heart, like yours. She went to school and knew languages, law, and she studied the Qur'an.'

The waiter turned up again to clean the table next to them, and they again fell silent. She saw his skin was reddening around his nose and ears.

She took a sip of her tea.

'How old were you then?' she asked at last.

'Eight.'

'And your father?'

'I don't remember a thing about him. He had long annulled his marriage with my mother. She ran away from his home, in fact, when my younger sister was born.' Sumer didn't look at her, his fingers drumming the table. 'Her death pushed two of my siblings and me out to the streets, broken and penniless. My sister was adopted by a rich household, as a child or a wife—both, I guess. I had no choice. To feed myself and the one younger brother left by my side, we begged near the railway station and the mosque, but that wasn't enough. So I began stealing. When things got worse, I moved to a different slum along with my brother and there I met some boys who were older and stronger. They taught me the art of stealing and escaping,' he said, sipping at his tea.

'Then?'

'Even if I was an orphan, I knew I wasn't the only one deprived of food and home. More than half a million Afghans had evacuated their houses by then due to escalating conflicts between the Taliban, western forces and the government. People were moving to the slums on the outskirts of the city. Only a few had the money to flee to neighbouring countries like Pakistan; some, who were richer, fled to western countries as refugees.'

'How did you meet Haza?' Meera said.

'One night while we were stealing from the house of a rich Pathan on the upper side of Herat, the others fled over the wall and escaped while I got caught. It was then that I saw Haza for the first time; he was working for Pathan, running some errands. The Pathan handed me over to him like a jailer would hand over a thief to a jallad to be tortured.' An odd smile elongated his lips as he looked up. 'A short, frail kid, in ragged clothes and with hair full of dirt—I had no chance against Haza. He seemed as big and daunting as he had before his death. I cried like I'd been trained to while begging, but Haza didn't spare an inch of my body. The Pathan enjoyed my beating. When he was satisfied, he allowed Haza to take me away and throw my body outside the city. On the way out of Herat, while I was tied up in Haza's jeep, I imagined my end. The massive man would crush me under his feet and dump my body into the Hari River. But Haza had a different plan.'

'What plan?' Meera asked, restless.

'He took me to his house in Kandahar and fed me. I was shocked. I hadn't eaten such delicious food in years. While I was eating, I noticed his lavish house—the kind I'd only ever seen in movies. He had servants and cooks! He patted me on the back like he'd found a needle in a haystack, or a precious gem in a coal mine. He took me to a local seminary the next day and got me admitted there.'

'What about your brother? Did you just leave him on the streets?' she said.

He looked uneasily around the restaurant, and then turned back to Meera. 'I went back to look for him when I got a chance to step out of the seminary, but I couldn't find him.'

She placed a palm hesitantly on his as his eyes welled up. He looked at her hand and withdrew from her touch.

'He must've survived,' she said.

He said nothing.

'Come on,' she said, 'let's go.' She rose to leave, and he followed her out.

Twenty-two

Whenever Meera had thought of tranquillity, she was reminded of the tiny village of Chamasari in the Doon Valley. It occupied her mind—the place where she had been born and raised, her true soil, just as Herat was for Sumer. Now, as they trotted down the lesser-known streets of Kyelang, he explained to her the simplicity and exquisiteness of his home town, where his maternal uncles had farms and grew pistachios, saffron and sometimes grapes, all to be sold in the town of Sufian outside Herat. She looked at him, startled by his warmth, as if he was a new man entirely. He went on, telling her about the tender minarets, the lush vegetation and the beautiful mountains surrounding his village.

She settled down on the platform stretching beneath a closed store as flurries of snow began to swell up in numbers and obstruct vision. The tarpaulin sheet overhead, although sloped, was quickly weighed down as the snow heaped upon it.

'We're so close to the safe house!' he said, standing in front and throwing his hands up.

She peered into the storm. The purple sky was turning

greyish. 'I don't want to go in. It's suffocating. Give me fifteen more minutes,' she said.

He sat down beside her and followed her gaze.

'Did you ever feel like running away from the seminary Haza had put you in? Was it suffocating?' she asked, looking at him.

'No. I shared a room with ten other boys, all of whom were staying at the madrasa and were the same age as me. The school had all that I desired: three meals a day, clean clothes and safety.'

'Like home?'

He smiled, and Meera noticed that an expression of profound happiness suddenly crossed his face.

'Hafeez sahib—he was a decent man. He loved all the boys like his own. He had a good reputation in the neighbourhood and had taught at the seminary for years. He had a grip over language, history, calculus and grammar, but often struggled with science. To all my questions, he'd involve the Almighty instead of giving a real scientific theory, and I'd believe it,' he said, wearing a noticeable spark of amusement in his eyes. 'Haza used to pay frequent visits to the mosque and to the school. He'd check on my progress, test my knowledge of the Qur'an and the Prophet Muhammad. I'd answer most questions accurately, and he'd bring small gifts for all the children there. He had begun to feel less intimidating with time.'

'So, he was cultivating you? Of course, children are easy to manipulate.' Meera looked away.

'I don't know, but he saved me from dying in some filthy trench like my brother.' His eyes were fixed on the falling snow. 'As soon as I finished my basic education at Kandahar, he took me to a higher seminary, in the east. I was sad to lose my friends and the comfort of a smaller group, but I was also excited to see the big city. Before we left, Haza had told me all about the beauty of Kabul, about the gardens of Babur, the museums, palaces and advanced facilities...The new seminary was indeed bigger—and I mean in terms of the area it covered, the resources and influence. It had all the modern equipment necessary, from a chemistry lab to a shooting range; a playground, gymnasium and library, very similar to the Darul-Uloom-Haqqania in Pakistan.'

'Like a complete training institution,' Meera said. 'Who were your trainers?'

'Either fighters from the Afghan-Soviet war or instructors who'd harnessed those warriors. But they all had one motivation: to liberate Afghanistan from Soviet influence and its forces. My trainer, Abdul-Tawab, was regarded as the toughest of them all, and he would pay close attention to each one of us. Although his name suggests forgiveness, he wasn't forgiving at all. He hated mistakes, indiscipline, and above all, behaviour forbidden by the Qur'an. I attended his class along with forty other boys in the beginning. That number began to decline soon, based on our performance. Tawab was known for polishing just the diamonds. His previous students had earned names and titles in war, and we were expected to perform just as well.'

'What were your fellow students like?'

'The boys were either refugees or petty criminals, all abandoned by society, but Tawab said we were the chosen ones, soldiers of God. There were a few students from the

Philippines, Indonesia and Qatar, who were supposed to return to their countries and carry out operations across the border.'

Meera's expression shifted as she took in this information. 'What were your thoughts like? You knew what they were training you for, right?'

'The first class each day would be on awareness of and reverence for the Qur'an; it was led by a Sunni imam. His sole purpose was to influence and pump passion into our young heads, to the extent that even a privileged saint like you would lift a rifle and aim at an infidel. We had no contact with the world outside, not for over ten years. We didn't know much about right and wrong back then; we did what we were supposed to do. If we didn't, they'd put us in an isolation cell and begin a different kind of training. I used to miss Herat and my earlier life. I wrote to Hafeez sahib several times, but he was getting older and had begun to lose his memory. Haza was busy with other operations, regarding the reorganization of the Taliban after America's intrusion and the murder of its prominent leaders, but he visited me sometimes and treated me like his own son.

'I was growing and so was the faith of Tawab in me. I participated in a few insurgencies under his orders, and Tawab was impressed by my performance. He was a good friend of Haza's and would sometimes also treat me like his son, but that softness in his heart would go away once we started training.'

'What did they teach you?' Meera asked quietly.

'Everything we had to know in order to survive and fight in remote locations. There was a strict pattern to follow for exercise, dieting and combat drills. Tawab used to bring unloaded weapons to class to demonstrate their make, model and operation. He began with lighter weapons—the Webley MK IV pistol, for example—and then moved on to the AK-47 and AK-56 rifles. Each country has its own set of weapons, you understand. The Indian army, for example, uses the INSAS rifle, AK-47, AK-103, IMI sniper rifle and the NSV machine gun. The US uses different generations of the M16 rifle. Slowly, we were trained on real guns and, depending on our capabilities, we were segregated into groups. Some boys were trained to be snipers, some learned surveillance and spying, and those few who could grasp chemistry's complex equations, learned explosives.'

'And you were among those few.' Meera sighed.

'I'd always liked science. If I'd been born into a normal life like yours, I'd have studied something good.'

Meera peered into his blinking eyes, trying to work out what she saw there. After a moment, she said, 'I liked science too, but I knew my father would not allow me to learn aviation, so I left my passion to my brother. He's the pilot now.'

Sumer looked up. 'You're not happy with your life?'

'Sailing with the tide—yeah, it keeps me floating and safe, but I'm not sure if it'll take me to some place I actually want to go.' She smiled, captured some snowflakes and allowed them to settle in her hands. 'Truth is, I've taken so many visions from other people that I've forgotten my own.'

'At least it won't get you killed.' He chuckled.

She looked at his face intently. 'Why don't you quit this and start a different life?' she said, her voice more excited than she'd intended for it to be.

He gave her a small smile. 'You talk like a boy I knew at camp. Kamran. He was the most brilliant amongst us. He learned the Qur'an better than any of us. The captain believed in his ability to make the right decisions, and thus he asked him to lead the group during a minor collision with NATO soldiers near the Tajikistan border. At the site of the shooting, a few Afghans were killed alongside the American soldiers, and Kamran froze on the spot. We had to pull him out of the field. The captain was upset. When we returned to camp, he took Kamran out for a walk, said he wanted to speak to him in private. That was the last time we saw our friend… We heard a gunshot in the distance and knew Kamran was dead.' Sumer swallowed the lump in his throat. 'When we enter this world, we close all doors back to a normal life. I can't disappear. Whether the thickness of the soil or the vastness of the sky, nothing can keep me hidden.'

His face flushed. The wind played with his dark brown hair, and his eyes blankly gazed at the road. Meera sat quietly, her chin on her knees, her arms coiled around. The snowflakes began to feel heavy, and then at once felt static to her—as if they'd been suspended in air and time, working against the laws of physics and gravity. She wanted to say something, but realized that she'd slur all her words, or her tongue would simply freeze. She smiled sadly, realizing that she had never felt like this: like all her knowledge and judgements amounted to nothing.

Sumer rose, breaking her fixed gaze, and began walking towards the safe house. She followed close behind.

∞

The next day, Meera awoke at nine, and pulled aside the curtain at her window. The ground was covered in a white blanket of snow, and the tree trunks peeked out from under their crowns of white. Beyond the vibrant brown of the distant eroded hills, the entire scene was a blank canvas. Meera pressed her face into the glass of the windowpane, quivering at the sight of her first real snowfall.

The sound of her door suddenly being unlocked pulled her away from the window, and the curtain fell back. Sahil entered with a breakfast tray in his hands and laid it on the table near the door.

'Good morning,' she said.

The teenager glared at her. 'What's good about this morning? Emre is sick and I've to do all his work,' he said, keeping a hand upon his hip.

'What happened to him?' Meera asked.

'Fever,' he muttered. 'Isn't he soft? He does this every time; whenever we stay out for too long. He's the most excited at first, and then comes down with sickness within ten days. Even you're better than him.'

She looked at him, perplexed.

'I mean you never complain, no matter how we keep you,' he said, fumbling slightly.

She looked down, a subtle smile on her lips, and carved a figure on the ground with her foot. Sahil was already strolling around the room, checking the water in the jug and picking up dishes from yesterday, which Meera had already rinsed and laid to dry on the table.

'Okay, I should be leaving now. Will come around two o'clock. You've got everything for now,' he said. With a final nod, he headed out of the room. Meera heard the lock rotate on the other side of the door and listened as his footsteps faded away.

In the afternoon, just as Meera emerged from the shower, Sumer walked in and, muttering apologies, averted his gaze. Then, sitting on the futon, he looked to the other side of the room. His gaze held at the slightly pushed-back curtains.

'You were peeping outside?' he asked.

She'd finished straightening her clothes and was now untangling some knots in her damp hair. Her hands slowed and she gaped at the blank wood wall in front of her.

'No.'

He turned and stared at her. 'I saw you from outside.'

'I, uh…looked at the snow and wondered if you had gone running this morning,' she said, glancing at him.

'I didn't.'

'Can you take me out now?' she said, excitement creeping into her voice.

He watched her for a moment, her frame clad in simple clothes of earthy colours. Her large warm eyes were clear and calm, looking with tender friendliness at him. She was beautiful as the winter, from the delicacy of her face to the cuts and lines of her lean frame. He ran a hand across his mouth absently, and then his voice cracked with a strain.

'Let me fetch my gun and then we'll go.'

'I think most shops take money here,' she said.

He gawked at her. She saw him tapping his boot on the floor.

'I can't believe you're fidgeting about such a simple thing,' she said.

'I'm not fidgeting. I just can't take the risk,' he exclaimed.

'Living with explosives and gunpowder your whole life, you think humans are a risk?'

'Those things are predictable,' he said, looking at her.

'Humans are too—mostly.'

He looked at her, rubbing his chin.

'Okay, but you've got to be careful,' he said, relenting, and then stood up.

∞

Paths of loose snow imprinted with shoeprints led to the market, where only a few stores remained open. Meera covered herself with her shawl as her eyes ran in all directions. She kicked soft chunks of snow towards Sumer's feet as he walked in front of her. He turned around, stared at her, and carried on briskly.

She ran up the sloped road to catch up with him.

'We have to leave this place before another storm hits and we get stuck here,' Sumer said, not looking at her.

Meera struggled to catch her breath. 'But where will we go?'

'I don't know,' he said, looking at the closed shops.

'You don't want to tell me.'

'I told you all about me. Isn't that enough?' he said, audibly annoyed.

'I can't get it out of my head. Why did you tell me? More importantly, why do you trust me?' she said, halting in the middle of the road. She stared at him.

He sighed. 'Because I can see it in your eyes: the faith you have in me, and the faith that I have in you,' he murmured, turning around. 'I've killed people while they begged for their lives, but with you—I can't imagine hurting you.'

His light brown eyes narrowed as he peered into her eyes. She trembled, letting the shawl slip from her head and fall upon her shoulders.

'You should've left that day,' he said, drawing back his gaze.

She pulled the shawl back over her head. A light gust of wind sent dry snow scurrying across the ground. She shivered.

'With that man? The one who looked at me like Haza did?'

'He looks immoral, but he isn't. In fact, he graduated as a spy. He plays street characters, performing artists, beggars and sometimes vendors, all to run surveillance.'

'Why didn't you let me go alone?'

'Because you would've informed someone and had us traced. Hoque wanted to get rid of you and I convinced him to send you home with one of our men. By the time you'd have reached Delhi, we'd have gone far enough from Choupal in Sukhbir's jeep.'

She massaged her temple, doubts papering over curiosity.

'I screwed it up,' she said.

'Kind of. But it's still not late. You can leave. I'll go to the room and tell them you sneaked away.'

'What if they track me down and get to my family?'

'They won't—not if you remain silent.'

She inhaled, taking a long pause. 'Hoque will believe you?'

'He won't have a choice.'

'And how're you going to explain Haza's death to your higher-ups in Kabul? He was an important man,' she said slowly.

'Well...if I survive that long, I'll face them.'

'I heard Hoque and Sahil talking about it. They'll go against you if asked about Haza's death.'

'I know that.' He scoffed, but then his expression changed quickly. 'You should go. This place isn't safe for you.'

She blocked his way in the street. 'It's not safe for you either. We're leaving together.'

Sumer laughed, pushing her aside. 'Don't be naïve.'

'I'm serious. All this time, I've only been thinking about myself. I didn't realize that you saved me twice, expecting nothing in return. You were right: there's no price I can put on the faith that you have showed in me, nor on the fear that you've lived with all your life.'

He strode on, not turning.

'Let me settle the price of my release in another way. I'll help you start a new life. We'll figure out how to get you documents and a new identity—everything you need to live in India for a while, and then, if you want, you can move to some other country. Think about it. You won't have to live with compromises,' she said.

'Nonsensical. I told you, it's impossible.'

She slowed down, watching him hurry into the distance.

Twenty-three

Sumer walked in through the back door of the safe house. He halted, listening to the footsteps behind him. Meera followed him at a distance. Disappointment partly shadowed his face as he turned to stare at her. Once again, he had expected her to escape, but she hadn't. She paused before the threshold of the door, swallowed a lump, and eyeing him, walked inside. Her face showed nervousness, but she was adamant too.

Outside her room, Sumer pulled out a set of keys out from his pocket. But as he moved to unlock the door, he froze. The door was open, the lock mangled. He recoiled, gesturing for Meera to take cover around the corner. Then, he rushed to his room and returned with a pistol and pressed his back to the wall, ready to peek around the doorframe, gun held steady.

Meera kept her hand over her mouth, feeling her heart pounding in her chest. Sumer crouched, keeping his body away from the thin wooden door.

Then, interrupting the silence on both sides of the door, he announced, 'If something happens here, we are all in danger.'

No reply came.

'Hoque, you want one of us to end up like Haza? I understand you're doubtful at the moment, but nothing has changed. You're my brethren, and you have my word.'

'You can't fool us any more!' Hoque yelled from inside the room. 'If you want to prove your loyalty, kill her. Or we will kill you both.'

'Okay, let me in. We need to talk first,' Sumer said, moving closer to the door. 'I'm coming in. Let's talk.'

His hands trembled as he pushed the door with the tip of his pistol.

The hinge of the door creaked as the thin wooden flap moved inward. Sumer entered, crouched low and keeping his pistol steady. Three of his men faced him, rifles held high. Sumer aimed at Hoque, who stood between Emre and Sahil. Sumer glared at the teens. The boys, indecisive, glanced between him and Hoque.

'I'd very much like to take a bullet from my own blood rather than from an enemy, but that's not what we came here for,' Sumer said, his voice reaching out into the corridor. 'We're all meant to die, sooner or later; it's up to you to decide if you can accomplish this mission without me.' He paused and looked at Emre.

Hoque aimed at Sumer's head. 'What're you up to with that Hindu girl?' he shouted.

'She's just a girl—petrified and disgraced by Haza—what threat does she pose to you? If the law for zina had been carried out rightfully, Haza would've been stoned to death, and that would've settled his wrongdoing in the eyes of the Almighty. Now, as his apprentice, I can't do much except beg for remission from that girl and alleviate his soul from sins so he can find a place in another world.'

Hoque kept his gun steady, but the younger men lowered theirs, eyes continuing to dart back and forth.

'Taking her out in public? Is that a part of your process of remission? I see no fear on her face. Did you tell her everything?' Hoque shouted.

'If you believe that, then what're you waiting for?' Sumer said, his eyes burrowing into Hoque's. Slowly, he placed his pistol on the floor. 'We've already lost one man on this mission. Reinforcements are unlikely to arrive any time soon, especially now that we're so close to the valley.'

Hoque glared, his chest inflated, and his breath shook.

'You're not Pashtun like us. I don't know why they chose you,' he yelled.

Sumer stood straight, muttering, 'We're here to fight a national war; don't stoop so low.'

'Son of a bitch,' Hoque spat.

'Watch your mouth,' Sumer grunted and grabbed the barrel of Hoque's rifle, pushing it aside.

Hoque scoffed, glaring up into Sumer's face even as he was shoved back. 'Don't you know why they executed your mother, huh? She was faithless, just like her son!'

'She was innocent. Pigheads like you framed her because she questioned the law,' Sumer growled, grabbing the older man's collar.

Hoque yelled, shoving Sumer back, 'Cheating is in your blood, scoundrel!'

Sumer closed the gap quickly. He wrapped his hands around Hoque's neck. 'You tear this group apart for your own advantage, bastard. How dare you plan this? And for what? To take my position! I'm the only one here who has the information we need. You, though? None of us need an idiot like you around,' Sumer spat as Hoque struggled for breath.

'Allah knows you are a betrayer,' Hoque croaked, gasping for air.

'Leave him!' Meera yelled, bursting into the room, feeling a sudden surge of courage rise in her chest.

Everyone spun around to stare at her. She looked at the strewn pillows and broken mirror.

'Get out of my room! All of you, now!' she yelled.

Sumer let go of Hoque's neck. Hoque fell forward, sucking in air, glaring at Sumer.

'Did you go through my stuff? And spit in my room?' she questioned, striding around and then looking daggers at Emre and Sahil. 'Worse than animals!'

Emre pushed Sahil towards the door and they snuck out, taking their rifles with them. Hoque glared at Meera and, after a moment, walked out of the room, muttering to himself. Meera picked up the strewn cushions and turned the flipped furniture over before she began to clear her clothes from the ground.

∞

Evening arrived. Her thoughts were strewn about herself, much like the pillow fibres in her room. Sumer returned to Meera's room just as she'd finished restoring it to its earlier state. But the mediocre bed had lost one leg and the mattress had flopped to one side.

'They broke my bed,' she said.

He pawed wordlessly at his forehead. Meera lunged, pulling up the sagging plank while he crouched beneath, trying to realign the broken slat. An hour later, they supported the broken part using a heap of stones picked from the backyard. Sumer lay quietly on the ripped couch, pressing his temples.

Meera clambered up on a chair to fix the rod between the curtain brackets.

'What're you thinking?' she asked as Sumer continued to pound his forehead with his fingers.

He sang, and smirked to himself. '*Ye del mige beram beram, ye delam mige naram, naram.*'

'What does it mean?' she said, climbing down from the chair.

'It means, on the one hand, I want to go, but on the other, I don't,' he said, glancing at her. Insecurity streaked lightly upon his cold face, and the girl had witnessed it for the first time in days.

'We're heading to Kashmir,' he said in a low whisper.

'Okay.'

'I'd been warned about these dilemmas before heading to India. After all, Kashmir is not our war, it's Pakistan's.' He peered out of the window, his words becoming slower. 'Fighting NATO soldiers in Afghanistan is different. We wanted to free our land from foreigners, but in Kashmir… we're supposed to threaten ordinary people to leave their houses. It seems like nonsense.'

She looked at him as he sat up.

'Then don't go,' she said.

He sighed and looked at her. 'I wish it could be that simple.'

'Can I ask you something?' she said, looking away hesitantly. 'If your mission was Kashmir, why were you in Saharanpur, all the way in the east, robbing a tour bus?'

'It was a different operation earlier. You might not like to hear about it, but if Haza had succeeded in receiving a package, Haridwar would now be a real cemetery. We lost our connection and our supplies. Robbing became a necessity until we could reconnect with our unit for supplies.'

A wave of fright ran through her. 'Haridwar is forty miles away from my village. It's almost my home town,' she exclaimed.

'Kashmir is home to many people, too, and so was Herat when I was thrown out on the streets,' he said.

'I can't believe it.' She gasped and stood, pacing towards the window to fix the curtains nervously again. Her hands trembled as she tugged at the fabric, the vibrant roads of Haridwar flashing before her eyes. The image of children begging on its streets faded, and it merged with the image of children begging in the streets of Herat.

She looked out at the pale moon in the sky.

'Do you ever wonder what is beyond this universe?' she asked.

He looked at her, surprised.

'Like, we're on this earth, and this earth is in the Milky Way; the Milky Way is but one among a hundred billion other galaxies, and what is beyond that?'

'Some sort of energy,' he uttered, opening his eyes. Then, propping his back against the couch, he said, 'I wondered about this often when I was a kid, even asked Hafeez sahib. He said Allah lives in the skies up there. You can say Shiva.' He chuckled.

'No, seriously. Tell me.'

He snorted. 'How would I know? No one knows.'

And yet somehow, they all claim to know, she thought and looked at him and then back at the curtains, which were drifting back and forth, blocking the sight of the moon in the sky.

'When are we leaving for Kashmir?'

'The day after tomorrow, hopefully,' he said, rising from the couch. 'Okay, you should sleep now. Do not open the door for anyone—except me.'

She nodded as he left. The door closed, and she heard the key turn in the lock.

Twenty-four

The moon was bright in the Delhi sky, hidden behind clouds but still illuminating the cold night. Aniket gazed at it for longer than he had in several years. Perhaps he'd simply not given himself the time. *I've nothing left here,* he told himself, cupping his face between his palms as the night dragged on. He looked at his packed suitcases and the briefcase containing the papers for his house in the village—a letter of allotment and the final sale agreement between him and a local retailer. The price was far lower than what he'd projected to list for commercial buyers.

Sunny barged in. 'Bro, you flung your house in the hole. Why such haste?' he exclaimed.

'I couldn't think of anything better,' Aniket said, his voice heavy. 'Until now…I'd thought my family had made a mistake by leaving their country, but I realize now that, perhaps, they weren't entirely wrong.'

Sunny placed a warm hand upon Aniket's shoulder. 'You should go. You don't need to see this. I'll take care of it.'

Aniket looked up. He hadn't seen this mature and forgiving side of his friend in years.

'It would be such a relief to know the truth—even if she is no more, that would be better than not knowing anything at all,' he said. As he uttered the last word, his voice cracked, and he began to sob.

'We'll find out soon. This world isn't big enough to hide those motherfuckers,' Sunny said grimly, looking at the two big suitcases lying by the closet, partly packed.

'I should've never let her go to that doomed fucking... factory,' Aniket whimpered. He raised a fist and hit the side of his bed.

'It's not your fault.' Sunny sighed. 'When are you leaving?'

Aniket peered blankly out of the window. 'Sunday night.'

'Well, don't tell my mom.'

∞

The roads in Kyelang had been mostly cleared by the end of the second day, after the storm passed. Vendors and small entrepreneurs began to wind up their businesses to migrate to the foothills of the Himalayas, before transportation came to a standstill for winter and the town went into hibernation.

The troop packed their stuff and prepared to leave. Meera laid in her room, alongside her packed luggage, thinking of the ghastly things that could've happened the other day if she'd stepped into the room before Sumer and confronted Hoque. A strong wind thrust the windowpane open and the room filled with the fragrance of the snow-capped peaks. She closed her eyes, allowing the wind to bid her adieu.

She rose after a while and peeped outside. The snow was heaped on flat surfaces and the hills had a bluish tint to them. Clouds floated above them, and the villagers led yaks and buffalo herds from their pastures into their barns for the winter.

Sumer stepped into the room. 'Close the window.'

Meera quivered and pulled the curtains closed. 'I was just—'

'We're leaving now. Pick up your stuff, and put on several layers. Don't fall sick. Emre's fever was quite enough,' he said.

'Okay,' she mumbled, and then noticed the efforts he had made to improve his appearance: neat clothes, his hair trimmed and swept back, and a pleasant smell unlike the usual ferric and gunpowder odour.

She glanced into his brown eyes. 'Do you really want to go?'

He looked back at her, his eyebrows raised. After a moment, he sighed. Meera swore at herself inwardly; she'd underestimated his resignation to such quandaries.

'I gave you a choice to leave, and I can still cover for you if you set off now,' he said, stepping forward. 'Staying here won't end well for you. Hoque proposed using you for our mission this morning. You know what that means: putting some damned explosives on you and…I cannot keep fooling them about what I feel for you for too long,' Sumer said.

She stared at him. He squinted, blinked swiftly, and then his eyes turned blank. He rubbed his face with his palms and exhaled. The sound of footsteps approaching outside the door shook him from his stupor.

'Emre and Sahil are waiting outside; they'll take you to the end of the street. You've got ten minutes to clear out of the place. There's a jeep waiting for us.'

With that, he turned and marched out.

Meera watched him go. A cold wind swept through the open door.

∞

Kyelang to Purthi, via Sazar, Pochal and Chingam. The troop finally emerged from the Himalayas and entered Kashmir in yet another stolen police jeep. The new driver didn't seem to have a name—or perhaps, Meera thought, he had adopted so many fake identities that he didn't remember his real name any more. Hoque called him 'Ustad'. Apparently, he was a local protester who'd been working with indigenous Kashmiri groups for twenty years; he had been arrested several times. The residents of Chingam called him 'Psycho', but he called himself a descendant of God sent to fight for the freedom of those weaklings who feared losing their wives and children.

The further the group moved north, the easier it became for the boys to blend in with the natives. The Kashmiri people too had light skin tones, long noses and bluish-green or hazel-coloured eyes. Moreover, Hoque had an accent—he'd spent many years in the valley, and he spent much of the journey talking to Ustad about the locale and its people.

'Kashmir is cold too but, unlike Afghanistan, it doesn't see droughts for months,' Sahil said, joining Ustad and Hoque's conversation as the jeep continued along the highway.

Hoque, who had been cheerful since the morning, glanced around at everyone and said, 'It's magnetic every time you visit.'

'There's a reason everyone wants it, my boy,' Ustad said,

grinning. 'Even Emperor Jehangir praised the beauty of this land: *Gar firdaus bar-rue zamin ast, hamin asto*'

'*Hamin asto, hamin asto,*' Emre completed the rest.

'If there's a heaven on Earth, this is it, this is it,' Ustad said. The boys behind him peered out at the lake, mountains and the sheep grazing on the hills.

Meera kept glancing at Sumer; her unease grew. Finally, she closed her eyes, unable to stop thinking of what could lie ahead: the side of Sumer she didn't want to see about to unfold in front of her. Mixed feelings flooded through her. Vulnerability and uncertainty welled up in the form of tears, which rolled down her cheeks. She turned away, sparing Emre and Sahil the sight.

After nine hours spent travelling through the highlands, they arrived at last at a makeshift camp on the outskirts of Chingam village, which Ustad referred to as his current dwelling, put together after dozens of raids of his earlier camps by the Indian army. He turned off the jeep's engine between a cluster of tents, all attached low to the ground and coated with dry leaves. Cedar and oak trees sprouted in between the tents, giving it the impression of a natural forest. A group of people emerged to greet the captain. Ustad introduced Hoque and Sumer to the other men. Startled by the presence of a woman, the men at the camp approached hesitantly.

Hoque suddenly walked ahead, spotting a familiar face among the crowd.

'Sarfaraz!' he shouted and made his way towards the grinning man. The two embraced and fell immediately into a warm, laughing conversation. Sarfaraz was an old friend of Hoque's from the Kabul seminary he'd attended. He'd been his roommate and had been trained as a sniper alongside him. Sahil followed Hoque and Sarfaraz into one of the tents while Emre and Meera stayed with Sumer and listened to Ustad as he explained the rules of the camp.

∞

As the only woman, Meera was pushed into helping Emre prepare dinner in the camp's temporary kitchen, which had been carefully constructed so as to control the flow of smoke and the fragrance of food into the jungle. She glanced at Ustad's nephew, Naji, a flimsy teenager who helped with the pantry.

'You've got to keep an eye on food rations as supplies arrive only once every fifteen days,' Naji said, placing the ladle in the pan before him and looking at Emre. Emre nodded while laying down several metal mugs upon the plain rock that the insurgents used as a table.

Naji continued, hardly looking at the woman. 'I'll be heading home early today. I've got to study for a test in the morning.'

'You go to school?' Meera asked.

The young boy looked at her for the first time, evidently startled; vapours from the hot pan rose into the air, forming thin shadows upon the far wall.

'Hmm,' Naji replied, looking down and stirring the ladle.

Meera marvelled at the boy's coldness, which perhaps echoed the silences that followed the ongoing battles tearing his homeland apart. Three wars, and a dozen scuffles between India and Pakistan had churned hatred among the native

Kashmiris, who wished for nothing more than freedom from both nations. Meera could thus understand the boy's hesitation; she wouldn't trust outsiders either if she were in his position. The boy turned off the gas fire and walked out of the kitchen.

'Is he coming back?' Meera asked Emre.

'I don't think so. He's going home,' he said.

Meera tried to reposition the pan and struggled with the shaking equipment. Emre harshly put down the mugs and snatched the pan away from her.

'They think you know everything!' he said. 'But look, you can barely hold a pan.'

'My mother used to cook,' she said.

He scoffed. 'What did you do then?'

She spoke at once defensively. 'I worked in an office. I handle data, watch files, process cheques worth many lakhs.'

He frowned. 'You mean you've never cooked?'

'I can make tea and smoothies if you've got a blender,' she said, blushing.

'Ah, a blender—in the jungle! I'm impressed.' Emre scoffed, pouring the soup into mugs.

'I was going to learn,' she muttered.

'You can't fill your stomach on your own? Embarrassing. Look at all those "animals" who're better than you.'

'You're crossing the line,' she whined.

He laughed. 'Go tell your *boss*!'

Sumer strode into their tent and glared at them both.

'What're you doing? They're waiting for food. All the lights have to go off before sunset,' he grunted.

Emre hurriedly finished pouring the soup into the metal

mugs as Meera said, 'It's ready.'

∞

The night grew dark and the camp sank into the obscurity of the forest. The wind swirled around the tall oak trees and pushed dry leaves over the ground. The gusts shook the thin walls of the tent. Meera lay awake on her mattress, a flashlight clutched to her chest. Every now and then, she'd use it to check her surroundings. One last time, she ran the light around her bed, then gently shifted it to look upon the faces of the sleeping Sumer and Emre in her tent. They snored, the sound deep and deadened.

She shivered, envying their ability to adapt to whatever cold dungeon presented itself. She tried to stop thinking about what could be out there—snakes, wild dogs, leopards, bears—and, of course, the Indian army, who might just figure out where another of Ustad's hideouts were and kill her along with the militants. She lay back on the mattress and continued to toss and turn, shaking under the thin blanket. Her feet, frozen, popped suddenly out of a hole in the blanket and hit Emre.

He sprang up in his sleep.

'Something touched my feet!' the boy exclaimed.

'Where did it go?' Sumer chimed, awake, turning on the flashlight.

'Some animal sniffed its cold nostril on my feet—or maybe, it's a snake,' Emre said, as Sumer peered around the tent, still half-conscious.

Meera sat up. 'They were my feet.'

Sumer swept his flashlight over her, and she squinted in the light.

'Daft. Why did you do that?' Emre grunted.

'This blanket has a head-sized hole. I'm freezing. I can't sleep in this.'

'Okay,' Sumer said.

Emre exclaimed, 'But she touched me!'

'It was barely a tap!' Meera said.

'Okay, stop it!' Sumer yelled. 'You'll switch positions, and if I hear anything more, I'll throw you both out of this tent.'

'Good. Sleep in this cold bed and then you'll see,' Meera said, rising from her bedding.

Emre scowled. 'It's cold in my bed too. That's because we're not in a hotel. It's a jungle, princess!'

'I said, not a word!' Sumer shouted as the two switched positions and glared at one another from across the tent.

Meera slipped inside the new bed as Sumer switched off his flashlight. Across the tent, Emre turned and coiled his hands around his knees.

'You're freezing,' Sumer said softly, touching Meera's forehead as she lay down next to him. He pulled her close, the blankets piling around them, and he pulled them up her shoulders. She shivered upon realizing that the distance between them in the blackness was thin as a hair. Her hand, cold and oblivious, had brushed against one of his fingers. She held her breath, her nerves working beyond their typical abilities.

She closed her eyes, trying to sleep as thoughts, somewhat alien and rebellious, raced inside her head. Her emotions, deepening, drew her entire consciousness towards the minuscule part of her hand that had touched Sumer's finger.

The wind blew at the tent walls, and the whisper of leaves playing on the ground outside reached her.

She flipped around to lie on her back.

Emre turned over and over in his bed, trying to sleep. Eventually, he gave up and kicked his blanket to the ground. Then, turning on his flashlight and draping Meera's shawl around his shoulder, he rose.

'I'll check with Sahil,' he said.

'Stay where you are,' Sumer grunted. 'It's your first day here and you're already fluttering like a fly in the middle of the night.'

But the boy walked out heedlessly and unzipped the tent's door. 'I know where Sahil is sleeping. I'll be careful,' he said. A gust of cold air forced itself inside.

Sumer rose and walked behind him angrily. 'Why does this boy test my patience?' he muttered. Emre jumped out and pulled the several flaps of the tent open.

'He's just a kid,' Meera said as Sumer watched him circling the camp cluelessly in his skinny pyjamas. Finally, someone let him into one of the other tents.

'These kids don't understand the seriousness of rules,' Sumer said.

'He's not in the right age to understand *anything*,' Meera said after a pause.

'I feel protective,' Sumer said, lying back in his place. 'If he's still alive, my younger brother will be about his age.'

Meera watched his face harden. After a moment, the light flickered off.

'You think about your brother every day?' she said in the dark.

'Not every day, but sometimes, I dream that I'm chasing him around the railway line and the mosque where we used to loiter,' he said quietly. 'He used to run so fast on his tiny legs. I had to keep an eye on him constantly.'

She placed her fingers mildly upon his head. He went silent, his breath heavy and slow; she knew she had crossed a line and it could yield any result now but also, she didn't want to think about it. She waited for him to speak, but nothing came out of his mouth. She pulled her hand back, her pulse elevated, and in the darkness, she shook her head, cursing herself.

He finally spoke, 'I wish we had met differently.'

She opened her eyes.

'As in?'

'I mean, at work or university,' Sumer said. 'I'd have fallen for you anywhere, as I was meant to. But then we would've dated, loved and fought, and, at the end, gotten married.'

'You wouldn't have looked at me. I'm so lame in real life,' she said, chuckling.

'You think so?' he said.

'I'm an introvert, and an average performer.' She turned towards him. 'People tell me if it weren't for my father, I'd have achieved nothing.'

'Everybody is born with different abilities and personalities. Why compare yourself with others, feel vulnerable and react?'

'What ability might I possess?' she said, a smirk forming on her face.

He laughed softly. 'Maybe you don't feel threatened, and that's how you survived here. If you had judged Hoque, you'd have died of a panic attack before he ever shot at you.'

'Or, I'm simply ignorant about his strength.'

'Better to recognize ignorance than to mistake it for certainty.'

She was quiet for a moment. 'Where did you learn to talk like this?' she taunted.

He didn't reply. She glided fingers across his forehead and then over his eyes.

'You're not scared of me?' he murmured, feeling her fingertips upon his nose.

'Maybe not,' she said.

Her fingers paused on his lips.

'What if it's a mistake?' he said.

'What if it's right?' she said, leaning over.

'You shouldn't trust me,' he murmured.

'I shouldn't listen to you.'

He pulled her to his chest and, in the cold night, she felt her skin burning, as if this entire complicated stretch of her life finally made sense. Her hair fell over his face and he brushed it aside, looking into her dark smouldering eyes; the fragile moonlight travelled through the tent's window.

The cold wind swept around the oak trees, and dry leaves piled against the tent, but neither of them felt the cold.

Twenty-five

Agony, when pushed too far, takes the shape of a revolution. That force can flip the most stable of monarchies, be it the British or the Mughal reign on the Indian subcontinent.

Meera was studying the Kashmir conflict through the eyes of Ustad, who deemed Azad Kashmir the only truth. He walked beside her, carrying a bulky AK-47 upon his shoulder, moving towards a nearby stream. She stood apart as he dipped a bucket into the fast-flowing brook.

'My girl, Kashmir belongs to Kashmiris, and no power can claim its soul,' Ustad said, handing the filled bucket to Meera.

'Why are we seeking help from Pakistan if we wish to see it free from both nations?' she spoke, passing him another bucket.

Ustad raised his eyebrows. 'The people of Kashmir pray to the same lord as us; the majority are Muslims,' he said.

'Just that?'

'When Kashmir was pressured to join one of the two new nations after Independence, the king of territory, Hari Singh wanted to remain isolated, like Nepal and Bhutan, but signed a standstill agreement with Pakistan so that the citizens, who were majority Muslims, could continue trading with and travelling to Pakistan. Soon, riots broke out in the valley as people demanded transparency regarding their status and a name for their land. The king turned to India for military help to curb the protests and India, cleverly playing its hand, agreed to help only if the king would annex Kashmir to the new India. Now tell me, my daughter, was that fair?' he said.

'Help comes at a cost, Ustad, and the king paid it,' Meera said, lifting two buckets as Ustad lifted the largest.

'But the people of Kashmir feel betrayed,' Ustad said, his eyes carefully observing Meera's expression.

She smiled and looked away. 'Indeed, it was a betrayal.'

∞

Sumer's group, along with a few of Ustad's men, gathered around a route map of Chingam village in a tent adjacent to the pantry. Meera stood close to the thin wall of the kitchen, listening in as she chopped the vegetables which would be used for lunch. Naji rinsed a pan alongside her, leaving the marinated meat to soak in herbs and spices.

Hoque's voice echoed from the tent as he proposed threatening a few influential Hindu and Sikh households in the village, which might work as a trigger to push the remaining infidels out. Sarfaraz agreed, going on to explain the specifics of the houses and fields surrounding the village.

'With changing trends, most people look alike—but I warn you, no Muslims should be hurt during the mission,' Sarfaraz said.

'We'll be shooting people?' rose Sahil's voice.

'Not until your leader says so,' Sarfaraz said. 'We'll move in three units. I'll lead one group in from the east. Hoque and Nadeem will take the west side. Hasan, you'll lead Emre and Sahil through the southern farms to the house of the Sikh landlord.'

'These Hindu and Sikh families are well sewn into Kashmir's culture, and you may come across a Muslim neighbour when you enter. Be careful who you target,' came another voice, one Meera didn't recognize.

'Emre and Sahil, when you enter this Sikh's house, you'll confront a sentry who sleeps between the garage and the porch to the north. He's Hindu; you can shoot him,' Ustad's voice said.

Inside the kitchen, Naji looked at Meera's ashen face and her trembling hands. She smiled suddenly upon catching his gaze and simply asked, 'How was your test?'

'It was okay,' he said, looking at her shaking fingers and the unevenly diced vegetables on the chopping board. 'You're sweating.'

She laughed softly. 'Oh, these onions…'

He turned around to pour oil into another pan. 'How long is it going to take?' he asked.

'Almost done.'

He lowered the flame under the pan, and walking out of the tent, said, 'Call me when you're done.'

She struggled with the knife until it slipped on an onion and sliced into her thumb. Blood dripped steadily from her hand. She recoiled, cursing under her breath, and ran to a nearby bucket of water. There, she cleaned the wound, blood and water mixing upon the earth below.

Sumer wandered in. 'Have you seen the matches?' he asked vacantly.

Meera looked at him, her breath inconsistent and her eyes welling.

He placed a cigarette between his lips and stepped close to her, eyeing her bleeding hand.

'They're all psychopaths, everyone, talking about some king and age-old revenge,' she said, shaking. 'Let's run away before we fall into the hands of these madmen. I don't care what they want to do with Kashmir; I just want to live, and with *you*.'

He stared at her.

'Listen to me, Sumer, they won't find out if we disappear tonight. Take me along to the village. Naji told me about the bus that arrives at the station around eight-thirty every night. It'll take us to Jammu.'

He looked surprised and then, holding her wounded hand, he looked into her faltering gaze, 'Your world will never accept me.'

'Your story is true and, if you surrender, the judge will reduce your sentence to only a few years. I'll be your alibi. You just need to expose Haza and everything will fall into place.' She gazed into his eyes, determined to make him understand.

He let out a bitter laugh. 'A few years? Let's count: for highway robbery between sunset and sunrise they'll sentence me up to fourteen years; kidnapping is another seven; a dozen murders? Let's say a hundred and twenty years. For terrorism and disruptive activities, I'll be detained for one year without trial, and then, for possession of firearms, ammunition and explosives, it's another twenty-five—so, even if you're my alibi and the judge is spellbound by my story, which he wouldn't be in the first place, because it's the story of every individual like me out there, I'm still looking at a hundred and seventy years of imprisonment.'

Meera swallowed the lump in her throat. 'All right, we won't surrender then; we'll just go away,' she said, sniffling. 'I know a place, in the east where I grew up, but we'll go even further. We'll forge documents and move out of India.'

He looked calmly at her face while she went on.

'People at the camp are already seeing through my origin story. If I keep fumbling, they'll know very soon that I'm not one of them. We don't have much time.'

He delicately tied a piece of cloth around her cut thumb. 'I've nothing to give you except my past, which will follow us, wherever we go. You're smart, young and deserve a good life.' Softly, he reached over and turned off the flame as the smell of burning oil rose from the pan.

'Why can't you be with me? Because I'm a Hindu, or is it because your mentor disgraced me?' she said.

'Because you're being silly. I can never give you the kind of life the other guy you're engaged to could,' he said.

'So, what about last night? You wanted me as much as I wanted you!'

'And I still want you, but do you want a terrorist? Marry a weapon? I can't give you a life because I take lives. Even if we escape these people at the camp and thrive without any money, I can't escape the fact that my conscience died long ago, when they killed my mother. It's too late for me to change. This feeling is within me now; I can always kill again.' His eyes filled with emotion. 'You're a diamond, and I'm a stone; one is meant to decorate, the other to throw.' He turned away.

'You'll die,' she said.

'At least I'll be honest to one world—*my world*,' he said.

'They'll never reward your honesty.'

'Neither will the people of your world,' he said. Then, with a final glance, he turned away from her and left the tent.

∞

That night, the family of the Sikh landlord witnessed the killing of his guard and a boy who happened to fall in Hasan and Sahil's way while they demanded the family to leave Kashmir. The other two units from the camp intimidated a few Hindus in their houses and fired in the air. News of the infiltration and shooting spread across the neighbourhood and, lashed with panic, Hindu and Sikh families sought shelter at their Muslim neighbours' houses. Sirens blared across the streets as people waited, silent, captive inside their houses.

The plan surfaced as anticipated: it triggered fear among minorities, challenged authorities who sent the town into lockdown. However, it failed to be accepted by the majority of Muslim residents of the valley. They cursed the immoral acts of the militants as vehemently as the others in town. Each one mourned the loss of the poor guard whose family had depended upon him for everything, the young son of the Sikh who had just returned home after finishing college and lastly, the Hindu entrepreneur, who'd run the sweet shop in the main arcade of the town for thirty years.

The next day, the situation at the camp deteriorated as the police began the hunt. Ustad stayed in his tent, quiet and profound, smoking handmade cigars. The day after the raid, he summoned Sahil. Sahil walked into the tent, expecting to be rewarded for his vital act.

'Salaam, Ustad,' the boy said, an arrogant smile playing on his lips.

'Wa-alaikum-salaam. Sit,' Ustad said evenly, the odour of his cigar lingering in the air.

The boy sat in a handmade bamboo stool placed across from Ustad's chair. Ustad looked down, and said in a gentle tone, 'What did Sarfaraz tell you about shooting?'

'He said I could shoot the guard,' Sahil said, the smile upon his face wavering.

'And what did you do?' Ustad said, looking up into the boy's face now.

'Shot the guard and…the boy.' Sahil's smile disappeared now. He swallowed the lump in his throat and glanced at the bulky AK-47 resting next to Ustad.

'You came here with fine references from Tawab, didn't you? Didn't he teach you that shooting an American soldier in Afghanistan is different from killing an unarmed civilian in Kashmir? It's a holy war; you win when you win its people over,' Ustad growled. 'I wouldn't have protested for twenty years if I could just put a bullet in the head of every infidel. In Kashmir, you hunt as much as you can eat, because leftovers draw vultures to you.'

The veins around Ustad's neck swelled as his eyes reddened. He rose and walked towards the boy.

'Ustad, I had no intention of shooting, but that Sikh boy lured me into a fight, saying that someone who had strength wouldn't creep around at night and attack an unarmed opponent,' Sahil said nervously.

'And your ego couldn't take it?'

Seizing the neckline of his sweater, Ustad pulled the boy from his seat and tossed him upon the ground. He crashed near Ustad's feet, like a small, dead animal.

'He lifted a knife too!'

'So you put three bullets in his head and jeopardized my camp?' Ustad yelled. 'Get out of my sight before I chop you into pieces.'

Sahil rose as tears of anger welled up in his eyes. He walked out, red-faced, gnashing his teeth, and stormed into his tent, where Sumer and Emre lay. Tears rolled down his face as they turned to face him, shocked.

'He has completely lost his mind!' Sahil yelled. 'Begging for twenty years—what he calls protesting—hasn't moved a single leaf in the valley. Who's he to teach me about fighting?' Sahil punched the base pole of the tent, and the canopy above shook.

'What's the matter?' Emre asked.

'Tell that lunatic Ustad that we weren't taught to beg. If really wants this land free, he should let us fight for it. Otherwise, he should call off this mission,' Sahil fumed.

'You shouldn't have shot that boy. The police and villagers will come sniffing for Ustad now. And besides, a cop from the robbery case is already after Ferihad,' Emre said, placing a hand on Sahil's shoulder.

'I don't care about the police. Ustad should've thought

about that earlier, much before he ever sought our help. We're the best-trained fighters in the whole fucking camp, and he wants us to kneel down in front of stupid villagers.'

'The best-trained fighter is the one who puts aside his feelings and self-esteem,' Sumer said. 'We're here to serve him, and that's it. It's his camp and his plan, and however he wants us to fight, we will.'

Sahil glared silently; his fists tight; tears leaving a wet path on his dry skin through his grime-streaked face. His lips were pressed together. He stood and, without a second glance, stormed out from the tent.

Sumer watched him go.

Twenty-six

If you happen to come across a bad spirit in the street, don't look back or it will follow you home. Her mother's advice echoed in Meera's head; it was the same line of thought that had kept her from wandering away from home as a child. She smiled to herself. The cluster of silver oaks towered above her as she headed towards the brook. *Advice for a child*, Meera thought. Now, as a grown-up, she knew better: bad spirits lived within people; they weren't ghastly things that roamed on the streets on their own.

Water flowed over the pebbles and small rocks, worn smooth by years of erosion. On the far side, she saw Sumer strolling and, without thinking, she took off her shoes and jumped into the water.

He turned at the sound of the splash and, spotting her, shifted as she waded across.

'You could have used the giant log across the stream a little further up,' he said, smirking as he helped her up to the bank on his side.

She blushed. 'I wanted to feel the water.'

He took her shoes from her. She dried herself upon the

grass and then sat beside Sumer. The sun was bright, and the cold wind was blocked by a dense shield of trees. Birds in the canopy began to shriek a cacophony, and a pair of eagles passed in the distant sky. Meera gazed up, then plucked a flat white pebble from the ground and lay it beside her.

'I thought you were changing. Why the violence last night?' she said softly, picking up another pebble from the brook and balancing it upon the previously laid one.

'The boys had to do what they're supposed to do,' he said, his voice hard.

She balanced a third pebble on the earlier two, refusing to meet his eyes. 'What're we going to do now?'

'I don't know.'

She added a fourth pebble to her creation and the bottom stone trembled. 'How am I going to balance it now?' she asked.

He gently pulled one of the stones out; the rest of structure trembled and balanced itself. 'You've picked the wrong one. Choose the right ones if you want balance.' He peered into her eyes.

A stray lock of hair fell across her face, coming to rest between her damp eyes. She stared at the pebbles, and the tiny twigs of grass that surrounded the structure.

Sumer pulled a slip of paper out from his pocket and, looking away from her, held it out.

'Read it,' he said.

She took the slip and peered at two series of numbers. One looked like a phone number, while the other was the length of a car's licence registration number.

She glanced up at Sumer, frowning. 'What is this?'

'Everything is going to change tonight, and no one—except

you and me—know that. Promise me, you'll do as I say,' he said.

A tear escaped her eye, but she held the rest in.

'I've thought a lot and realized it's never going to end. We need to escape. The phone number written there is the key. Ustad and all the others are packing to leave tonight as the police are searching for them in the vicinity. You'll go to the village and call this number. The man at the end of the line will ask you for a vehicle number and directions. You'll say this number and give him directions, which I'll give you by nine o'clock tonight as I don't yet know where Ustad is heading. After winding up the call, dispose off the cell phone and SIM card separately and wait for me.'

'Why? What're we going to do? Why should I go to the village?' she exclaimed.

He held her face in his palms. 'I'm leaving, just like you wanted, and this man will help us. Once this man does what I've told him to do, I'll get off the truck before the border and meet you at the village.'

'But who is he?' she asked.

'A friend,' he said.

She looked at him in disbelief. 'You'll seriously leave them and come with me?'

He nodded.

'And where will we go?'

'Leave it up to me,' he said, brushing an abandoned lock of hair away from her face. 'Just do as I say.'

The tears locked in her eyelashes rolled down. She threw her arms around his neck, her entire frame shivering.

∞

After following Naji stealthily through the jungle as he headed home, Meera finally arrived in the village. The atmosphere was quiet in the still-shaken shanty. The streets, normally occupied by chatting neighbours, were now empty, and only the sound of the wind and the barks of stray dogs split the silence. One such dog scrutinized Meera quietly from its warm corner. Lights blazed from several households, sharing their light with the otherwise dark street outside. Meera took the route towards the village periphery, just as Sumer had told her to, and reached a comparatively lively location: the highway, where buses from Jammu stopped a couple of times a day. Waiters strolled between tables in the roadside restaurant alongside it, taking orders from hungry passengers.

She looked around and pulled out the cell phone from her pocket. A male voice answered after the first ring, as if he'd been waiting for it. His voice was heavy and peculiar, Meera thought, though he didn't say much—she gave him the vehicle number and directions and he quickly hung up. *Sumer sure has some weird friends,* she thought to herself. Then, scraping the SIM card out of the cell phone's back, she threw the phone into a drain duct flowing out of the restaurant. Holding her bag and covering her face, she hurried inside the restaurant to wait for Sumer.

The furniture in the restaurant had seen better days. The bench that Meera settled down upon shook beneath her. Baked cookies and instant snacks stared at her from behind a glass screen, while the fragrance of freshly brewed tea hung in the air. She inhaled and held her breath, the scents mingling until she couldn't feel anything except the butterflies in her stomach. She glanced at the highway and then at the outdated clock hanging on the restaurant's wall. Her feet fidgeted beneath the bench, as she thought of her family. She wished she could tell them somehow that she was fine and happy. Closing her eyes, she imagined herself looking into Sumer's light brown eyes, saw their squint as she peeped into them, his charismatic smile blossoming below, disbelief playing there...

She hadn't felt this kind of exhilaration in a long time, perhaps not in years. Finally, she would possess something she desired—something that would change her fortune like magic.

She remained there, lost in her thoughts, smiling to herself. About an hour later, she noticed a man in the passenger lot watching her. She met his gaze and he began to walk towards her. She stared, trying to recognize his bawdy eyes, coarse beard and the black amulet hanging around his neck, but she failed. His clothes were dark, merging with the moonless night.

'Meera?' he enquired hesitantly. When she nodded, he handed her an envelope.

Confused, she smoothed it open and unfolded the letter within.

The man began to walk away, trying to disappear amidst the crowd of passengers.

By the time you finish reading this, you'd have already heard the explosion—a big cloud of fire forced by the energy of nitroglycerine and grain dust, a combination of chemicals that is neither hard to make nor to use. This time, though, I didn't make it myself; instead, I trusted this man, who just gave you this letter to make a good one, just for me. His mates would have chased and planted his creation upon my truck by now. Thus, having done what I couldn't do from inside the camp.

Meera rose, crushing the paper in her hands and looked desperately for the man who'd just handed her the letter. She pushed her way through the crowd, her body shaking, towards the highway, where he appeared—a mere shadow in the night, his shape moving towards Chingam village. She yelled at him, and the shadow stopped, turned, glanced back at her.

She ran with all the strength she had, but he was already running, disappearing into a grove of chinar trees.

Finally, Meera stopped. He was gone.

She slumped to the ground, gasping for breath. The wind was cold and the dry chinar leaves crackled around her in the quiet night. She searched inside her polybag and pulled out a flashlight and, trembling, she swept the light across the grove, hoping the shadow might reappear, but it was too late.

She peered down at the letter.

It's amazing. I've made these simple explosives a dozen times before, each with the strength to split rocks apart. I know for certain that it will crush my truck and tear all the human bodies within it to pieces.

The flashlight in her hand shook and her vision swam as tears dripped on to the letter, blurring the ink. She wiped her face frantically, trying to focus.

When we chose to walk this path, we accepted that we have to kill to remain alive, knowing that our ends have already been written and, by doing what we're told, we're only stealing a sliver of time from death's hand. When

Haza brought you here, I knew what was going to befall you, but I didn't have the strength to stand against him. Allah perhaps had wanted for us to confront his evil this time, and now that I've saved you, pulling you back into the darkness of my realm would bring me disgrace, and doom my eventual awakening. You may think I'm afraid of living, of loving—perhaps you're right. Perhaps living without these things for so long has left me with certain beliefs. I've seen good people die early, while the evil live to be old men. Everything I've cherished has been crushed whenever I dared to hold on to it. You would be too.

This war will not end as long as it benefits a few, but this explosion, at least, will release those caught in this endless circle—for this lifetime. Their beliefs will end with minimal pain. And odd pebbles will balance themselves again.

Sumer.

Far away, from the west side of the village, a dull boom echoed through the valley. Birds burst through from the canopies, shrieking into the cold night, and a giant ball of fire made its way from the earth to the sky. The still air trembled as shockwaves swept over each stone, pushing each dead leaf, every single atom aside; the sound resonated through the rolling hills. For a brief moment, the dark night shone brighter than the day, and then came the smoke. Meera fell.

Lives of all sorts began to surge, scream, bawl and look for shelter. Meera watched the smoke, motionless, numbed—her mind anaesthetized with shock and eyes incapable of blinking away.

Epilogue

About six years later...

Thin clouds blurred the sky of New York City, the weak sun beyond illuminating one of the last few summer days. The wind blew across the East River, shrewdly enfolding the warmth to hail the arriving cold. The yellow flowers of littleleaf linden paled beside colourful maple and planetree leaves, and in the cafes and restaurants, pumpkin spiced lattes and turkeys replaced summertime offerings.

Aniket closed his laptop and pressed his hands over his eyes. It had been a long day. His forehead ached, and he took a deep breath and held it. The sun peeped through the horizontal blinds covering his office window, bathing his face in light. When he finally opened his eyes, it was almost 5 p.m. He rose groggily from his desk, turned off the light, and headed out. It was time to call it a day.

The sun was lower in the sky by the time he arrived outside a house. It was a huge detached thing in South Hempstead, overlooking the island on one side and the wide sky on the other; it calmed him every time he came to see it. The grass was framed by rocks on both sides of the pavement, which led to a shaded patio. He observed several new stones there; they hadn't been there a month ago.

In the living room, he laid a champagne bottle on the table.

'You didn't dress up?' he said, finding Meera watering plants in the backyard.

She turned, windswept hair in curls, skin radiant around her creased and smiling eyes. She rubbed her face upon her sleeve and pushed aside her hair. The small scar on the side of her ear was as fresh as it had been six years ago, when she had returned home, from what had become an unexplained part of her life for her family— and the wider world.

Meera hurried as she spoke. 'You said the guests will arrive by seven-thirty. I still have time.'

Aniket looked around the house and clapped. 'Well, it's six, and I see nothing has been done.'

'Ahmm, you can move the furniture around and hang some lights in the living room. I've ordered food; the cake should be delivered soon. What else do we need?' she said, throwing her hands above her shoulders.

Aniket chuckled. 'Meera, your daughter asked for a jungle-themed birthday party in clear words! Be ready to handle her tantrums now.'

A carton full of Christmas lights from last year rested near the kitchen. Aniket opened the box and sighed. 'These aren't even close to the fairy lights she asked for.'

Meera shook her head from across the lawn.

A little girl sprinted through the front door in muddy shoes and ran towards the back of the house. She laughed upon seeing Aniket and climbed into his arms. Her hair was separated into two braids, escaping the elastic ties to erupt all around her head. Her eyes, light brown just like those of her father's—Sumer's—friskily turned to the champagne bottle.

She wiggled her hand to grab at it.

Aniket laughed, preventing her hands from reaching the bottle. 'It's not for you, little monster.'

'Where's my birthday gift, uncle?' the girl asked.

'We're bringing it. It's on its way,' Meera snapped as the girl struggled, still reaching for the bottle.

'Meera, leave your garden—go dress up. The kids are on their way and I can see very well that your neighbour's kid is sprinting here in an elephant costume from across the street.'

'Just a minute,' she said, sprinkling the last patch of grass before turning off the hose. This done, she knelt down next to the girl, easing off the child's muddy shoes. 'Stop fidgeting!' she said, smiling. Free from her shoes at last, the girl ran, giggling, back to her room.

Aniket peered into Meera's peaceful eyes. She met his gaze with a shy smile, coy even now, but she said nothing.

Meera rinsed her hands under the kitchen tap. Aniket sat beside the box full of string lights and began to untangle them.

'Did you get a call from your dad?' he enquired softly.

Meera rolled her eyes. 'I cannot make everyone like me.' She paused, took a deep breath. 'Mom called, and I spoke to Sunny. He might pay us a visit next month,' she completed her sentence and smiled.

'I wish your dad could see you doing so well. My firm wouldn't have been able to thrive this quarter without you,' he said, sorting out the lights.

She tilted her head and smiled. 'And I wouldn't have been able to do anything without a friend like you.'

∞

Later that night, when the house was still, Meera snuck out from the sleeping girl's room and walked to the balcony. She lit a cigarette, took a deep breath, and stared out at the wide sky, the stars and a bright half-moon above the dark ocean. Party lights from her living room caught in the shifting smoke of her cigarette, and she took another soft puff, feeling its fragrance and heat in her mouth—just like Sumer had taught her.

The wind was cold, but Meera let it hold her. She could taste the fragrance of the salt and the sea, and feel the tranquillity of her home. The curled locks of her hair played with the breeze until the gust slipped into the partly open window of her daughter's room. The chiffon curtains smoothly swam back and forth in the wind before settling and merging into the night's peace once more.

The wind caressed Meera's face, and then drifted towards the island, catching with it what might have been forever between the wide sky and the waving sea.